Six Kinds of Sky

Six Kinds of Sky

A COLLECTION OF SHORT FICTION

LUIS ALBERTO URREA

CINCO PUNTOS PRESS . EL PASO

Grateful acknowledgment is made to the following magazines and books in which these stories appeared: *Blue Mesa Review, The Guadalupe Review, The Long Story, Mirrors Beneath the Earth* (edited by Ray Gonzalez, Curbstone Press, 1992), and *Ghost Sickness* (Cinco Puntos Press, 1997). Portions of "Taped to the Sky" were also published in *The Arizona Republic*.

"A Day in the Life" first appeared in *By the Lake of Sleeping Children* (Anchor, 1996) and is used by permission of Anchor Books, a division of Random House.

Library of Congress Cataloging-in-Publication Data

Urrea, Luis Alberto.
    Six kinds of sky : a collection of short fiction / by Luis Alberto
    Urrea.—1st ed.
        p. cm.
    Contents: Mr. Mendoza's paintbrush — Taped to the sky — First
    light — A day in the life — Father returns from the mountain —
    Bid farewell to her many horses.
    ISBN 0-938317-63-6 (pbk.)
        1. Mexico—Social life and customs—Fiction. 2. Indians of
    North America—Fiction. 3. Mexican Americans—Fiction. I.
    Title.
    PS3571.R74 S59 2002
    813'.54—dc21

                                                        2001053908

Cover image copyright © 2002 by Miguel Escobedo
Inset image copyright © 2002 by Steve Rossman
Cover design by Vicki Trego Hill

Many thanks to those who labored with us
to publish *Six Kinds of Sky*:
Jonathan Gonzalez, Mary Fountaine, Susie Byrd, Eddie Holland,
Jessica Powers & Rus Bradburd.
(What did Rus do? Nothing, really.) Forget Rus.

ACKNOWLEDGMENTS

My first and best reader is my bride, Cinderella. First in everything. Everything, always.

Thanks to Dr. Joseph Gigante, without whose care it would have been impossible to complete this book.

Duane Brewer was the first to read "Bid Farewell to Her Many Horses." He took me into his circle, into Pine Ridge, and into his sweat lodge. The best moments in the Sioux stories are because of him. Mike Her Many Horses was kind enough not to kick my ass for borrowing his family's honorable name. Uncle Douglas White, Oglala Lakota medicine man, kept me in his prayers in a dangerous season. The comment about Butte La Rose in "Taped to the Sky" was first spoken by the inimitable Vickie Lloyd from down around the levee in Acadiana.

Thanks to the Byrd clan; to César A. González and the students of Chicano Studies at San Diego Mesa College; to Stewart O'Nan, who reminds me to keep it alive. To Gary and Stephanie Holthaus. To Brian Andrew Laird. To Bella Luna Books. And to that vato loco, Tijerina. Greetings to Mario and the Latin Kings, Chicago.

To Rosario, Sinaloa; to Tijuana, B.C.; to the American Road; to Pine Ridge, South Dakota—holy and beautiful; to Paris et Provence: Thank you.

This book is dedicated to my family—

Cinderella
Eric
Megan
& Rosario Teresa

CONTENTS

MR. MENDOZA'S PAINTBRUSH

WHEN I REMEMBER my village, I remember the color green. A green that is rich, perhaps too rich, and almost bubbling with humidity and the smell of mangos. I remember heat, the sweet sweat of young girls that collected on my upper lip as we kissed behind the dance stand in the town square. I remember days of nothing and rainstorms, dreaming of making love while walking around the *plazuela*, admiring Mr. Mendoza's portraits of the mayor and the police chief, and saying dashing things to the girls. They, of course, walked in the opposite direction, followed closely by their unsympathetic aunts, which was only decent. Looking back, I wonder if perhaps saying those dashing things was better than making love.

Mr. Mendoza wielded his paintbrush there for thirty years. I can still remember the old women muttering bad things about him on their way to market. This was nothing extraordinary. The old women muttered bad things about most of us at one time or another, especially when they were on their way to market at dawn, double file, dark shawls pulled tight around their faces, to buy pots of warm milk with the cows' hairs still floating in them. Later in the day, after their cups of coffee with a bit of this hairy milk (strained through an old cloth) and many spoonfuls of sugar, only then did they begin to concede the better points of the populace. Except for Mr. Mendoza.

Mr. Mendoza had taken the controversial position that he was the Graffiti King of All Mexico. But we didn't want a graffiti king.

My village is named El Rosario. Perhaps being named after a rosary was what gave us our sense of importance, a sense that we from Rosario were blessed among people, allowed certain dispensations. The name itself came from a Spanish monk—or was it a Spanish soldier—named Bonifacio Rojas who broke his rosary, and the beads cascaded over the ground. Kneeling to pick them up, he said a brief prayer asking the Good Lord to direct him to the beads. Like all good Catholics, he offered the Lord a deal: if you give me my beads back, I will give you a cathedral on the spot. The Good Lord sent down St. Elmo's fire, and directly beneath that, the beads. Bonifacio got a taste of the Lord's wit, however, when he found an endless river of silver directly beneath the beads. It happened in 1655, the third of August. A Saturday.

The church was built, obliterating the ruins of an Indian settlement, and Rosario became the center of the Chametla province. For some reason, the monks who followed Bonifacio took to burying each other in the cathedral's thick adobe walls. Some mysterious element in our soil mummifies monks, and they stood in the walls for five hundred years. Now that the walls are crumbling, though, monks pop out with dry grins about once a year.

When I was young, there was a two-year lull in the gradual revelation of monks. We were certain that the hidden fathers had all been expelled from the walls. A thunderclap proved us wrong.

Our rainy season begins on the sixth of June, without fail. This year, however, the rain was a day late, and the resulting thunderclap that announced the storm was so explosive that windows cracked on our street. Burros on the outskirts burst open their stalls and charged through town throwing kicks right and left. People near the river swore their chickens laid square eggs. The immense frightfulness of this celestial apocalypse was blamed years afterward for gout, diarrhea, birthmarks, drunkenness and those mysterious female aches nobody could define but everyone named "*dolencias*." There was one other victim of the thunderclap—the remaining church tower split apart and dropped a fat slab of clay into the road. In the morning, my cousin Jaime and I were thrilled to find a mummified hand rising from the rubble, one saffron finger aimed at the sky.

"An evangelist," I said.

"Even in death," he said.

We moved around the pile to see the rest of him. We were startled to find a message painted on the monk's chest:

HOW DO YOU LIKE ME NOW?
DEFLATED! DEFLATE
YOUR POMP OR FLOAT AWAY!

"Mr. Mendoza," I said.

"He's everywhere," Jaime said.

ON THE ROAD that runs north from Escuinapa to my village, there is a sign that says:

ROSARIO POP. 8000

Below that, in Mr. Mendoza's meticulous scrawl:

NO INTELLIGENT LIFE FOR 100 KILOMETERS.

There is a very tall bridge at the edge of town that spans the Baluarte river. Once, my cousin Jaime said, a young man sat on the railing trading friendly insults with his friends. His sweetheart was a gentle girl from a nice family. She was wearing a white blouse that day. She ran up to him to give him a hug, but instead she knocked him from his perch, and he fell, arms and legs thrown open to the wind. They had to hold her back, or she would have joined him. He called her name all the way down, like a lost love letter spinning in the wind.

No one ever found the body. They say she left town and married. She had seven sons, and each one was named after her dead lover. Her husband left her. Near this fatal spot on the bridge, Mr. Mendoza suggested that we:

UPEND HYPOCRITES TODAY.

Across town from the bridge, there is a gray whorehouse next to the cemetery. This allows the good citizens of the village to avoid the subjects of death and sex at the same time. On the wall facing the street, the message:

TURN YOUR PRIDE ON ITS BACK
AND COUNT ITS WIGGLY FEET.

On the stone wall that grows out of the cobble street in front of the cemetery, a new announcement appeared:

MENDOZA NEVER SLEPT HERE.

What the hell did he mean by that? There was much debate in our bars over that one. Did Mr. Mendoza mean this literally, that he had never napped between the crumbling stones? Well, so what? Who would?

No, others argued. He meant it philosophically—that Mr. Mendoza was claiming he'd never die. This was most infuriating. Police Chief Reyes wanted to know, "Who does Mr. Mendoza think he is?"

Mr. Mendoza, skulking outside the door, called in, "I'll tell you! I think I'm Mendoza, that's who! But who—or what—are you!"

His feet could be heard trotting away in the dark.

Mr. Mendoza never wrote obscenities. He was far too moral for that. In fact, he had been known to graffito malefactors as though they were road signs. Once, Mr. Mendoza's epochal paintbrush fell on me.

It was in summer, in the month of August, Bonifacio's month.

August is hot in Rosario, so hot that snapping turtles have been cooked by sitting in shallow water. Their green flesh turns gray and peels away to float down the eternal Baluarte. I always intended to follow the Baluarte downstream, for it carried hundreds of interesting items during flood-times, and I was certain that somewhere farther down there was a resting place for it all. The river seemed, at times, to be on a mad shopping spree, taking from the land anything it fancied. Mundane things such as trees, chickens, cows, shot past regularly. But marvelous things floated there, too: a green De Soto with its lights on, a washing machine with a religious statue in it as though the saint were piloting a circular boat, a blond wig that looked like a giant squid, a mysterious star-shaped object barely visible under the surface.

The Baluarte held me in its sway. I swam in it, fished and caught turtles in it. I dreamed of the distant bend in the river where I could find all these floating things collected in neat stacks, and perhaps a galleon full of rubies, and perhaps a damp yet lovely fifteen-year-old girl in a red dress to rescue, and all of it speckled with little gray specks of turtle skin.

Sadly for me, I found out that the river only led to swamps that oozed out to the sea. All those treasures were lost forever, and I had to seek a new kind of magic from my river. Which is precisely where Mr. Mendoza found me, on the banks of the post-magical Baluarte, lying in the mud with Jaime, gazing through a stand of reeds at some new magic.

Girls. We had discovered girls. And a group of these recently discovered creatures was going from the preparatory school's sweltering rooms to the river for a bath. They had their spot, a shielded kink in the river bank that had a natural screen of trees and reeds and a sloping sandy bank. Jaime and I knew that we were about to make one of the greatest discoveries in recent history, and we'd be able to report to the men what we'd found out.

"Wait until they hear about this," I whispered.

"It's a new world," he replied.

We inserted ourselves in the reeds, ignoring the mud soaking our knees. We could barely contain our longing and emotion. When the girls began to strip off their uniforms, revealing slips, then bright white bras and big cotton underpants, I thought I would sob.

"I can't," I said, "believe it."

"History in the making," he said.

The bras came off. They dove in.

"Before us is everything we've always wanted," I said.

"Life itself," he said.

"Oh, you beautiful girls!" I whispered.

"Oh, you girls of my dreams!" said he, and Mr. Mendoza's claws sank into our shoulders.

We were dragged a hundred meters upriver, all the while being berated without mercy: "Tartars!" he shouted. "Peeping Toms! Flesh chasers! Disrespectors of privacy!"

I would have laughed if I had not seen Mr. Mendoza's awful paintbrush standing in a freshly opened can of black paint.

"Oh oh," I said.

"We're finished," said Jaime.

Mr. Mendoza threw me down and sat on me. The man was skinny. He was bony, yet I could not buck him off. I bounced like one of those thunderstruck burros, and he rode me with aplomb.

He attacked Jaime's face, painting:

I AM FILTHY.

He then peeled off Jaime's shirt and adorned his chest with:

I LIVE FOR SEX AND THRILLS.

He then yanked off Jaime's pants and decorated his rump with:

KICK ME HARD.

I was next.

On my face:

PERVERT.

On my chest:

MOTHER IS BLUE WITH SHAME.

On my rump:

THIS IS WHAT I AM.

I suddenly realized that the girls from the river had quickly dressed themselves and were giggling at me as I jumped around naked. It was unfair! Then, to make matters worse, Mr. Mendoza proceeded to chase us through town while people laughed at us and called out embarrassing weights and measures.

We plotted our revenge for two weeks, then forgot about it. In fact, Jaime's "I LIVE FOR SEX" made him somewhat of a celebrity, that phrase being very macho. He was often known after that day as "El Sexi." In fact, years later, he would marry one of the very girls we had been spying on.

There was only one satisfaction for me in the whole sad affair: the utter disappearance of the street of my naked humiliation.

YEARS AFTER BONIFACIO built his church in Rosario, and after he had died and was safely tucked away in the church walls (until 1958, when he fell out on my uncle Jorge), the mines got established as a going concern. Each vein of silver seemed to lead to another. The whole area was a network of ore-bearing arteries.

Tunnels were dug and forgotten as each vein played out and forked off. Often, miners would break through a wall of rock only to find themselves in an abandoned mineshaft going in the other direction. Sometimes they'd find skeletons. Once they swore they'd encountered a giant spider that caught bats in its vast web. Many of these mine shafts filled with seepage from the river, forming underground lagoons that had fat white frogs in them and an albino alligator that floated in the dark water waiting for hapless miners to stumble and fall in.

Some of these tunnels snaked under the village. At times, with a whump, sections of Rosario vanished. Happily, I watched the street Mr. Mendoza had chased me down drop from sight after a quick shudder. A store and six houses dropped as one. I was particularly glad to see Antonia Borrego vanish with a startled look while sitting on her porch yelling insults at me. Her voice rose to a horrified screech that echoed loudly underground as she went down. When she was finally pulled out (by block and tackle, the sow), she was all wrinkled from the smelly water, and her hair was alive with squirming white pollywogs.

After the street vanished, my view of El Yauco was clear and unobstructed. El Yauco is the mountain that stands across the Baluarte from Rosario. The top of it looks like the profile of John F. Kennedy in repose. The only flaw in this geographic wonder is that the nose is upside-down.

Once, when Jaime and I had painfully struggled to the summit to investigate the nose, we found this message:

MOTHER NATURE HAS NO RESPECT FOR YANQUI PRESIDENTS EITHER!

Nothing, though, could prepare us for the furor over his next series of messages. It began with a piglet running through town one Sunday. On its flanks, in perfect cursive script:

Mendoza goes to heaven on Tuesday.

On a fence:

MENDOZA ESCAPES THIS HELLHOLE.

On my father's car:

I'VE HAD ENOUGH!
I'M LEAVING!

Rumors flew. For some reason, the arguments were fierce, impassioned, and there were any number of fistfights over Mr.

Mendoza's latest. Was he going to kill himself? Was he dying? Was he to be abducted by flying saucers or carried aloft by angels? The people who were convinced the old "MENDOZA NEVER SLEPT HERE" was a strictly philosophical text were convinced he was indeed going to commit suicide. There was a secret that showed in their faces—they were actually hoping he'd kill himself, just to maintain the status quo, just to ensure that everyone died.

Rumors about his health washed through town: cancer, madness (well, we all knew that), demonic possession, the evil eye, a black magic curse that included love potions and slow-acting poisons, and the dreaded syphilis. Some of the local smart alecks called the whorehouse "Heaven," but Mr. Mendoza was far too moral to even go in there, much less advertise it all over town.

I worked in Crispin's bar, taking orders and carrying trays of beer bottles. I heard every theory. The syphilis one really appealed to me because young follows always love the gruesome and lurid, and it sounded so nasty, having to do, as it did, with the nether regions.

"Syphilis makes it fall off," Jaime explained.

I didn't want him to know I wasn't sure which "it" fell off, if it was it, or some other "it." To be macho, you must already know everything, know it so well that you're already bored by the knowledge.

"Yes, I said, wearily, "it certainly does."

"Right off," he marveled.

"To the street," I concluded.

Well, that very night, that night of the Heavenly Theories, Mr. Mendoza came into the bar. The men stopped all their arguing and immediately taunted him: "Oh look! Saint Mendoza is here!" "Hey, Mendoza! Seen any angels lately?" He only smirked. Then, squaring his slender shoulders, he walked, erect, to the bar.

"Boy," he said to me. "A beer."

As I handed him the bottle, I wanted to confess: *I will change my ways! I will never peep at girls again!*

He turned and faced the crowd and gulped down his beer,

emptying the entire bottle without coming up for air. When the last of the foam ran from its mouth, he slammed the bottle on the counter and said, "Ah!" Then he belched. Loudly. This greatly offended the gathered men, and they admonished him. But he ignored them, crying out, "What do you think of that! Eh? The belch is the cry of the water-buffalo, the hog. I give it to you because it is the only philosophy you can understand!"

More offended still, the crowd began to mumble.

Mr. Mendoza turned to me and said, "I see there are many wiggly feet present."

"The man's insane," said Crispin.

Mr. Mendoza continued: "Social change and the nipping at complacent buttocks was my calling on earth. Who among you can deny that I and my brush are a perfect marriage? Who among you can hope to do more with a brush than I?"

He pulled the brush from under his coat. Several men shied away.

"I tell you now," he said. "Here is the key to Heaven."

He nodded to me once, and strode toward the door. Just before he passed into the night, he said, "My work is finished."

TUESDAY MORNING we were up at dawn. Jaime had discovered a chink in fat Antonia's new roof. Through it, we could look down into her bedroom. We watched her dress. She moved in billows, like a meaty raincloud. "In a way," I whispered, "it has its charm."

"A bountiful harvest," Jaime said condescendingly.

After this ritual, we climbed down to the street. We heard the voices, saw people heading for the town square. Suddenly, we remembered. "Today!" we cried in unison.

The ever-growing throng was following Mr. Mendoza. His startling shock of white hair was bright against his dark skin. He wore a dusty black suit, his funeral suit. He walked into a corner of the square, knelt down and pried the lid off a fresh can of paint. He produced the paintbrush with a flourish and held it up for all to see. There was an appreciative mumble from the crowd, a smattering of applause. He turned to the can, dipped the brush in the paint. There was a hush. Mr. Mendoza painted a black swirl on the flagstones. He went around and around with the legendary brush, filling in the swirl until it was a solid black O. Then, with a grin, with a virtuoso's mastery, he jerked his brush straight up, leaving a solid, glistening pole of wet paint standing in the air. We gasped. We clapped. Mr. Mendoza painted a horizontal line, connected to the first at a ninety degree angle. We cheered. We whistled. He painted up, across, up, across, until he was reaching over his head. It was obvious soon enough. We applauded again, this time with feeling. Mr. Mendoza turned to look at us and waved once—whether in farewell or terse dismissal we'll never know—then raised one foot and placed it on the first horizontal. No, we said. He stepped up. Fat Antonia fainted. The boys all tried to look up her dress when she fell, but Jaime and I were very macho because we'd seen it already. Still, Mr. Mendoza rose. He painted his way up, the angle of the stairway carrying him out of the *plazuela* and across town, over Bonifacio's crumbling church, over the cemetery where he had never slept and would apparently never sleep. Crispin did good business selling beers to the crowd. Mr. Mendoza, now small as a high-flying crow, climbed higher, over the Batuarte and its deadly bridge, over El Yauco and Kennedy's inverted nose, almost out of sight. The stairway wavered like smoke in the breeze. People were getting bored, and they began to wander off, back to work, back to the rumors. That evening, Jaime and I went back to fat Antonia's roof.

It happened on June fifth of that year. That night, at midnight, the rains came. By morning, the paint had washed away.

TAPED TO THE SKY

There is one way you could make me
completely happy, my love: die.
—Jaime Sabinas

I. KEEP HONKING

"HEY, BOO," the waitress said. "What you know good?"

She was being folkloric. Hubbard was supposed to be charmed. But since the demise of his Previous Marriage, about five and a half days ago, he'd been sullen. He once read about a Sioux warrior named Cranky Man, and now he thought: *That's me.*

Lafayette, Louisiana was as hot as the inside of your mouth.

"I don't know a damn thing," he said.

"I don't know me too," she replied, not taking to his Yankee-ass tone at all. "But hey, I'm just trailer trash from Butte La Rose."

A little dark guy in a red gimme cap snorted and nodded his head.

"Bon," he murmured.

She tossed him a smile and moved a hip in his direction.

Hubbard leaned an elbow on his little round table. It had gold foil ashtrays, with the corners sort of bent down to hold the smokes. Hubbard didn't smoke.

The waitress raised an eyebrow at him.

"Beer?" he asked.

She answered with her chewing gum as she turned away: Pop! Pop!

The guy in the red cap said, "She just trying to be friendly."

Boo. Hubbard had read that Louisiana women called you "sugar," but nobody had called him that. This was the second time, though, that he'd been called "boo." In James Lee Burke books, men called each other "podnah." But when Red Cap sidled up to Hubbard, he said, "Hey, asshole."

The waitress sashayed back to him and landed a cold Abita on a napkin; she moved away like a strangely reproachful dance. Hubbard sipped the beer. It was delicious. He gulped another mouthful of it.

"You're not from around here," Red Cap said.

"Just passing through."

"They teach you manners where you from?"

Hubbard was thinking: *Language is the enemy.* He and his wife had been speaking some debased lingo for years now. Hubbard wanted silence.

"Nope," he said.

"Ah," Red Cap breathed. "You a comedian."

Hubbard had spent the morning staring at bull gators in Lake Martin. He'd bought a gator fang from a Chittimacha artist at a Cajun dance festival, and he wore it around his neck on a black thong. Channeling some of that alligator hoodoo. He was Not Afraid.

"See that sign out there?" Red Cap said.

Hubbard craned around and looked out the smoky window. The sign said: POO YI!

"Poo yee?" Hubbard said.

"Poo yi. Rhymes with eye. That's 100% Acadian."

Hubbard gawked at the Spanish moss fogging up the sugar pines and cedars across the oyster shell parking lot.

"You speak French?" Red Cap asked. Hubbard drank some beer, shook his head. Red Cap smiled like an angel, said: "That sign, you could put it in English to say, 'Great American Ass-Kicking Center.'"

"Oh," said Hubbard. "You doing the ass-kicking?"

Beau Jocque and the Zydeco High Rollers were on the juke.

The guy grinned some more.

"Might do."

Beau Jocque sang, "Can you really make it stink?"

Hubbard drained his beer and said, "I could give a shit. I'm going to Texas."

After a while, Red Cap said, "Podnah, no wonder you in a bad mood."

HUBBARD WATCHED two Klansmen duke it out in Vidor, Texas. He could tell one of them was in the Klan because he had a blue KKK tattooed on his left arm. The other fellow wore a stars'n'bars Confederate t-shirt. Hubbard was deeply gratified to see he had a stark SS insignia inked on the side of his neck. Hubbard sucked on a banana Slurpee and hid among a hooting crowd of teenagers as the mullet hairdos of the fighters flung sweat and blood.

HE PILOTED HIS WIFE'S Volvo west. I-10 across Texas to the San Antonio cutoff. He took a room in a motel right at the split. Fort Something. The vapor lamps in the parking lot turned his skin pale purple.

Stinkbugs were swarming the lot, humping each other like horny army tanks, crackling under the Volvo's tires like pecan shells. Their pungent stench permeated the whole complex. Hubbard had a ground floor, and ecstatic stinkbug menages tumbled about before the door. He hauled his duffel to room 182 and toed the hard-shell lovers aside. A woman in the open door next to his smiled at him. Purple hotpants (those lights again). He spent seven seconds daydreaming that she was a hooker and he had $50 he didn't want but that she'd been so taken with him that she'd given him some lovin' for free. He was right at the part where he spent the $50 on supper and wine when a man reached out through the door and pulled her in. Slam.

Hubbard worked his key-card and got through without allowing too many stinkbug invaders to rush in. He threw himself upon the bed: it was about as comfortable as a cardboard carton. He spied a Xeroxed menu from the Fort Something Pizza Palace, *We Deliver to YOUR Room!* He ordered spaghetti. When it came, it was accompanied in its styrofoam boat by a side order of mashed potatoes and gravy.

Afterwards, he watched Letterman with the sound turned low so he could appreciate the ridiculous opera of passion coming through the wall: the gal in hotpants called out, "Junior! Oh my God, Junior!"

Hubbard's wife had never once cried *Oh my God.*

AT LAS CRUCES, he decided to turn north. I-25. He'd been eating breakfast in El Paso, reading a paper with little transparent grease-windows stained into the pages. Chorizo, huevos, frijoles, migas and coffee. The paper said there was a trailer park serial killer in El-ephant Butte, halfway to Truth or Consequences. A trailer park, incidentally, built on the site of a thermal pool where Cochise used to soak his aching bones.

Hubbard then left the Mexican diner and crossed the street to a deserty cemetery. He jumped over the wall and found John Wesley Hardin's grave. Murdering son of a bitch. He picked up a pebble from the pistoleer's grave and dropped it in his pocket.

Now he was headed into Billy the Kid's New Mexico. He could go up to Golden and visit Buffalo Bill. And up to Boulder and visit Tom Horn. Gunman graves. He was still in his deadly mood—he was on a killtour of the American West.

Elephant Butte reflected red serial killer bloodlight onto its somnolent reservoir.

Through Truth or Consequences. To Albuquerque. Beyond the west end of town, on the way to Rio Puerco, he stopped in a cowboy bar. He danced with a Navajo woman whose husband's feet hurt too much from diabetes to dance. They cut a rug to "Rock Lobster" and some Joe Ely and a Willie tune or two. After the dancing, they stood out in the parking lot and let the sweat dry.

"What are you?" she asked.

"I'm just a white boy."

"Oh," she said. "I thought you was a Leo."

Santa Fe, Las Vegas. A carload of fat Chicanos and Apaches offered to kick his ass at the gas station/drive thru liquor store in Raton. But he had already survived the threats of Red Cap at Poo-Yi. Screw the aggrieved minority contingent. He dove into the Volvo and tooled up the Raton Pass. He rose in that tan station wagon until he passed into the mystical vistas of Colorado. A sky so cheesy and refulgent that it could have been clipped from a Maxfield Parrish calendar.

HE WAS LOOKING at everything. Being married was like being dead! Like being in some trance! He'd been a gray man in a gray world! By God, the world was full of color!

Delightful Trinidad: filthy train cars banged through downtown. Blighted Pueblo: black slag and some sort of roadside fiberglass creature shop. Deer, elk, horses, burros, cows, lions, bears, bison stood as if frozen in a flash ice-storm, staring at the onrushing traffic. Republican Colorado Springs: insane Christian conspiracy theorists and the last hippies taking to the hills.

Hubbard pulled into Garden of the Gods. He was astounded by the red rocks, thinking his wife would really love this place. Then remembering to forget his fucking wife. He would not even think her name.

Then he cried.

THE CAR DIED on a two-lane angling northeast toward Fort Laramie, Wyoming. Visions of cavalry and Indian chiefs danced in his head: treaties, Red Cloud, Dull Knife. Then the car hollered at him and gave up a scent not unlike the reek of the crushed stink-bugs in Texas.

Hubbard wrenched the wheel to the side and ratcheted onto the shoulder. He sat there, ass-numb and back-sore, and looked stupidly at the speedometer. It continued to read "0," no matter how long he stared.

"Come on," he said. "Now what," he said.

He tried the ignition. Tried it again. Ghastly yowls as from a coyote with its leg caught in a steel trap.

"Okay," he said, believing this would lead to some decisive action.

Nothing happened.

He set the parking brake. Changed gears and changed them back. Got out, walked around the car, peered underneath it, looking for—what. He didn't know what he was looking for. Grease or smoke or something. There was some smoke, actually. It was blue. Cars were not his thing, especially not this piece of shit '87 car of hers. He got back in. The radio was still playing. Shouldn't the radio die if the engine breaks? Dr. Laura was insulting a man whose mother-in-law had fed his baby daughter Beano to stop her from farting. Dr. Laura was of the opinion that this man was weak. Hubbard punched in another station. Somebody wanted to know, "Who let the dogs out? Woof! Woof! Woof!" He turned the radio off.

"Let's try it again, shall we?" he muttered.

Crank. Yowl. Smoke.

HE SAT ON THE HOOD, resting his back on the windshield. The heat of the dead engine felt good—the Wyoming wind was briskly exploring his body. His nipples were as hard as his John Wesley Hardin pebble. He sipped some water from a bottle with French writing on the label. He ate M&M's—peanut. *Protein.*

Barbed wire twinkled like spiderwebs and dew. The sky went all the way down. He'd never seen so much sky. It went up one side of the world and cut an arc to the other side and seemed to attach itself to the horizon, as if the little sage bushes out toward Nebraska were buttons.

No cars happened along. He'd thought a rancher, a cowboy, somebody. A plastic bag danced through the weeds like Casper the Friendly Ghost.

"That's just great," Hubbard noted.

PERHAPS HE WOULD DIE out here.

Suicide was still not out of the question.

Or exposure.

Starvation.

He slid off the hood. Maybe she had some candy bars stashed in the glove compartment. She used to crack him up every time she said the best medication for PMS was chocolate. That bitch!

The chairman of her Cambridge AA meeting had been coming around their apartment. Like a total sap, Hubbard had even made this loser his famous ground turkey chili. It was all supposed to be "recovery" stuff, "working the steps," taking some sort of "inventory" together. That debased English he was cringing about. He used to speak good ol' American. He used to eat fried frigging pork. No more euphemistic holism! No more kashi! No more tofu hot dogs! No more professional sane-persons hugging him all the time!

Inventories. That Cantabrigian twelve-stepper had stepped right into Mrs. Hubbard's pants and taken a very personal inventory, indeed. And one day, when Hubbard came home from his teaching job, he noted her Sting CDs missing from the shelf. And her kitchen CD boombox. He looked in the bedroom—the bed was stripped. He said, "You've got to be kidding me." He hurried to the bathroom, knowing that if the Tampax was gone, she had run off with that sobriety pimp. The tampons were gone.

He used to like to tell this joke: the alcoholic comes home and says, What have we got to eat? His wife says, Two eggs. He says, Great—scramble me one and fry the other. She cooks the eggs and serves them to him. He shouts, Damn it! You fried the wrong egg!

She didn't think it was all that funny.

She left a note full of jejune natterings like *true love* and *karma* and *old souls* and something called the *earth school*. That one sounded like bootcamp for worms.

It was Hubbard's turn not to laugh.

A GESTURE was called for.

He skulked over to the AA pimp's Somerville flat and swiped

his wife's car. Then he purged his savings and burned south out of Boston. Bosstown. Beantown. Inane thoughts skittering around inside his head. His Rabbit was still parked in front of their apartment. He assumed she would drive it. But she could have gone to the cops—he could be a wanted man. Desperado. Outlaw. Bad mammajamma.

"Grand Theft, Aut-o!" he crowed.

For about an hour, he thought of himself as Grand Theft Otto. Aerosmith on the deck fueled his fantasy: "I'm baaaaaaaack in the saddle again!" Away, past refineries and airports, parkways and scattered woods. Mindless groundhogs beheld his passage. Bikers with CHINGALING on their backs gave him the finger south of NYC.

Virginia was a blur of shadows and a hallucinatory midnight amusement park, glowing white in dense fog. In the Carolinas, he enjoyed tobacco company smokestacks painted to look like gargantuan filter cigarettes.

Florida was his destination. He didn't care about Miami, Disneyworld, the Keys. He was feeling primordial, reptilian in his rage. He was a wild car thief. He belonged in a swamp. He aimed himself at the Okefenokee like a pistol. Pogo territory. Spiders as big as your hand, cottonmouths, malaria. Crazy dark continent dreams, a vanishing act. He bought a baseball cap with a gator on it: FLORIDA YARD DOG.

He slapped a bumper sticker on his wife's Easy Does It/One Day At A Time bumper: KEEP HONKING, I'M RELOADING.

One swamp wasn't enough—that swamp drove him to the mother of all swamps, the Atchafalaya. He floored it west through Bama and Mississippi, counting burst armadillos beside the road, thinking: *Lynyrd Skynyrd crashed around here.* And, crossing into Louisiana: *They ambushed Bonnie and Clyde in some of these bushes.* A hail of machinegun bullets, that was the way to end a love story, not a bare bed, missing tampons, and panties tucked in your front pocket. *Where'd those come from?* he wondered, fondling them with one hand as he steered between semis with the other. More stupid thoughts.

The occult Atchafalaya finally opened before him: dark water, vast white birds, lonesome cypress knees sticking out of the water like headstones.

Her panties. He was certain that, at any point along the road, he could throw them away.

A CLOUD MOVED OUT of Colorado and evaporated in the Wyoming sky.

Hubbard popped open her glove box, and a map, a hair brush, three hair scrunchies, and a wad of bills and papers fell out. A book of matches, Chapstick. She had a regular 7-11 in there. He came across one of the missing tampons: sudden memory flash of her challenging him to insert it, foot up on the toilet lid, him down on his knees, wielding the cardboard tube with a certain queasiness—he was afraid he was going to pinch something, tear her somehow. "Go on," she'd said, "I won't break." He tossed the tampon in the back seat. Aha—a Hershey bar, limp from the heat of the engine. But chocolate nonetheless.

And then he found it. The baggie full of pills. A rainbow of capsules and tablets: pink ones, blue ones, a black one, some red ones. White tabs of X. Well, well, well. Well, as the bluesmen said, well, well. That lying little AA tramp! Recovery, eh? Twelve steps, eh? Couples therapy, Al-Anon, sponsors, boring little recovery books cluttering their lives—and all the while she had a stash hidden in her car.

He fell back in the seat. He was done in. He laughed. He slapped his own head.

"Too much!" he cried.

After a while, he decided, *To hell with it.* The whole deal was a farce, all of it. He gobbled the pills and washed them down with the last of his French water. He got out again, took a last bite of chocolate, and arrayed himself on the cooling hood. Prepared to die.

II. SERENITY CONTRACT

DON HER MANY HORSES was on his way from Pine Ridge to Boulder. The crazy dudes of the Oyate organization at CU were throwing a party. It was a theme bash. They were calling it Dances With Nerds. You were supposed to come as the biggest dweeb you could imagine.

He spied the tan Volvo on the shoulder. A white guy was asleep on the hood. What's the deal with white guys, anyway? They'll try to get a suntan anywhere, anytime.

Horses slowed and stared as he passed, his head clicking in small increments like the Terminator. About fifty yards down the road, he stopped. He watched Hubbard in the rearview mirror, what he could see of Hubbard, which was a splayed pair of feet in red Converse hi-tops. Horses put it in reverse and backed up. He came even with Hubbard and pushed the window button. The window whined down. "How," said Horses. He loved saying that to white guys.

"Huh?" said Hubbard. He cracked his eye. He thought he saw a fish swimming over the road. He focused on Horses and his pickup. It was the biggest pickup Hubbard had ever seen. An extended cab 4WD Ford 350, fire engine red.

"That's some truck," he croaked.

"You all right?" Horses said.

"Not exactly," Hubbard said. Fish, he was sure of it, over there in the cottonwood. "Car broke."

Horses hung his head out the window and looked the Volvo up and down. A thick braid tumbled out and hung there. Hubbard blinked at it. *I'm not dead yet*, he noticed.

"Let's take a look," Horses said.

"Gee, could you?"

Hubbard thought, *I said, "Gee!"*

Horses glanced at Hubbard and thought: *Gee?*

Don Her Many Horses put down one size thirteen black cowboy boot. Through his wobbling daze, Hubbard noted the white stitching.

Horses reached back into the truck and extracted a big black cavalry hat. It had a high crown and an ample, down-curving brim. Braided horsehair band, big black and white feathers hanging off the back on some kind of strings. Crossed lanyards or whatever on the brim with beads, some cavalry thing. Why would an Indian want to wear a cavalry hat? Somebody else could ask Horses that. He was big. Big enough that Hubbard immediately tried to find ways to be ingratiating.

"Nice hat," he said.

Horses walked past him, saying nothing.

He rested his fists on his hips and observed the landscape. He didn't seem to be in any particular hurry to rescue Hubbard and get the car rolling again. "Pronghorn," he said. Hubbard squinted. He didn't see anything. "Over there." *Oh great.* Over there was about 1,200 square miles of plains and prairies: missile silos, coyotes, farm houses, pumpjacks sipping up crude oil, wrecked cars, tractors, power towers, interstates, cows. Hubbard couldn't be expected to see a pronghorn on such short notice. Preparations needed to be made.

"I mean, really," he said.

"What?"

Hubbard waved his hand to show Horses it was nothing.

"He's watching us," Horses said.

"I see him," Hubbard lied.

"You stretch out in the grass, he won't be able to help himself. He'll come over and have a look."

"You know it!" Hubbard exulted.

Fish, maybe seals. Eels in the tide of the air.

Horses said, "Watch this." He took off his hat and waved it. Suddenly, like a tawny ICBM, the antelope leapt straight in the air, lifting off from the ground and rising so high even Hubbard could see him. He pogoed away, bouncing through the high grass and casting disappointed glances over his shoulder.

"Hey!" Hubbard cried. "Cool!"

"Yeah," said Horses. "I should get out my rifle."

Hubbard looked at the truck: a fat rifle rested in a back window rack.

"A pronghorn steak marinated in wild blueberries. That's what's cool."

Horses shook a Marlboro out of a crumpled box and stuck it in his mouth.

"Smoke too much," he said. He fired it up, took a drag, and politely angled the smoke in a thin jet over Hubbard's head.

"That a bear tooth?" he asked.

Hubbard fingered his thong.

"Gator," he said.

Horses fished a chain out from under his shirt.

"Bear claw," he said. "Griz."

Hubbard didn't know what he was supposed to do. Drop trou and compare scars? He hung his thumbs in his belt and tried to look manly. His eyeballs jittered.

"How about that car?" he said.

"The car?" said Horses, looking at it. "It's a Volvo."

Hubbard just stared at him.

White guys, Horses thought, *aren't all that funny.*

WHILE DON HER MANY HORSES tried the ignition and listened to the screech, Hubbard's pills kicked off like cheap July 4th fireworks. He bounced in place, his hi-tops full of Flubber. His mouth came alive. It stampeded. He was suddenly in some Bugs Bunny cartoon, where the simpleton farmer or hunter is hexed and his mouth talks all by itself, and even though he's pressing both hands to his lips, they squeeze through his fingers and keep talking, talking and spitting, rubbery tongue doing the boogie in the air, habbala-babbala-boo!

"Boo!" he said. "They call you boo in Louisiana!"

"Really."

"And podnah!"

"No kidding."

"Yeah, right, right, right."

"Huh. Hows about that."

Horses stretched his back.

"Your car's broke, all right," he said.

"It's not my car, not really, though I paid for the goddamned thing so it should be my frigging car. I paid for everything."

Horses crossed his arms and settled in for the story. This one should be good. He leaned his butt on the fender. Crossed his ankles. Tapped the roadway with one heel.

"You paid every cent," he prodded.

"Right, right, yes. Put her through *grad school,* how do you like that, paid for five years' worth of *therapy.*"

Horses listened. Hubbard nattered. The whole sad story tumbled out.

"You ever been in therapy? Probably not! Can you believe this shit? We'd even," Hubbard announced, "made out a serenity contract."

Horses was already getting bored with this crapola. He started moseying around the Volvo again, sniffing, looking.

"Whatever that's supposed to be!" Hubbard called out.

"Pop the hood latch," Horses said.

Hubbard reached in and yanked the handle.

"Oh," he said, "I suppose it was all inner-child related."

"Inner child."

"Right. That's it. Isn't that pathetic? My inner child had issues, I suppose, with abandonment, etc., etc., et al, ad nauseum."

Horses raised the hood and braced it on its metal stanchion.

"Your inner child?" he said. "What are you, pregnant?"

Then he said: Haw!

He stepped away from the car laughing, and then he stepped back to the car, still laughing. Haw! Haw! He raised his hands as if warding off a blow. Don Her Many Horses was really enjoying that joke.

"Just funnin'," he said.

Hubbard was rendered silent.

Horses peered into the engine compartment.

"Hang on," he said.

He pulled out the oil dipstick.

"Got a rag?" he asked.

Hubbard pulled out his wife's panties.

Horses said, "Jesus Christ!"

Later, at the Oyate party, he'd be able to inform them: *The white man will show you his wife's underpants.*

"Put that away!"

Hubbard stuffed them back in his pocket.

But Horses didn't need a rag after all. The dipstick was clean and shiny. Horses brandished it in Hubbard's face like a fencer approaching with a foil.

"Look at that."

"So?" said Hubbard.

"No oil."

"So?"

"So when's the last time you checked your oil?"

"I didn't check my oil."

"You didn't check your oil?"

"Why would I check my oil? This is, like, a Volvo!"

"You drove ten thousand miles and never checked your oil?"

Hubbard said, "I suppose I might have."

"Are you out of your mind?"

No wonder this guy's wife left him.

"I'll tell you what, kola. This here engine's just about toasted."

Hubbard drawled, "Sucker's dead, is it?"

"Graveyard dead."

WHAT DON HER MANY HORSES did not feel like doing was to give Hubbard a ride back to Colorado. He thought if he stalled long enough, somebody would come along. White Bread could hop in and be on his way.

Hubbard had started talking about his domestic crisis again.

"Look," Horses said, "you've got to get over it."

"It's only been a week! Not even a week!"

"Yeah, and a week should be long enough to figure out that your marriage was miserable. You came out ahead."

"Excuse me?"

"You're ahead. She set you free."

"*Free!*"

"She set your spirit free, man. You was dying, and she opened the door and told you to fly away. And where are you now? You're in Wyoming. You owe her."

Once again, Hubbard was silenced.

Horses might have seen a windshield sparkle to the south. Deliverance was at hand. Unless they didn't like Indians. They could refuse to stop. You never knew out here.

He was dismayed to see the sparkle veer to the left and move across the plains, raising a vague dust cloud.

"Mind if I borrow your rifle?" Hubbard blurted.

Horses blinked at him.

"Your rifle," Hubbard repeated. "Can I use it?"

Horses looked at the rifle, then back at Hubbard.

"I'm going to put the car out of its misery."

This was getting interesting after all. Horses had never seen a guy kill a car with a rifle. He imagined the hours of stories this knucklehead was giving him.

"You know how to work a rifle?" he asked.

"I got a marksmanship merit badge."

"He got a merit badge," Horses muttered.

Curiosity overcame prudence.

"This I've gotta see," Horses decided.

He retrieved the rifle, jacked a few rounds in.

"It's a thirty-thirty," he warned. "Going to kick." Hubbard nodded, took the rifle. "And one more thing," said Horses. "You even start to aim that thing in my direction, I'm going to start that truck over there and back over your ass. Three or four times."

He trotted to his Ford and locked himself in.

Hubbard sauntered to the Volvo and tried to control his weapon. It wobbled and drifted, but he braced it against his shoulder and was startled by the Crack! when he squeezed the trigger. A headlight exploded and the car rocked.

"Whoo-wee!" he hollered.

Horses sat in his truck and adjusted the side mirror so he could watch Hubbard.

Crack!

"That's what I'm talking about!" Hubbard shouted.

Tires deflated; stuffing flew from seats; body detailing peeled away and clattered.

Crack!

A RUSTED-OUT DATSUN happened along, going the opposite direction. Two skinny young cowboys filled the front seat with knees and elbows. They stopped in the road and gawked.

The driver rolled down his window and said, "Sir? What's the deal with this here?"

"Guy's killing his wife's car."

"What she do, run out on him?"

"Run out on him last week. Screwing her AA sponsor."

Crack!

The driver whistled.

"That can't be good," he noted.

The passenger craned around and said, "Sir? You think I might get a shot at that Volvo?"

"Why not," said Horses. "Step right up."

The entire white race has finally gone insane.

The young man got out of the Datsun and worked a straw hat onto his head. He spit once and strode over to Hubbard. Hubbard squinted at him, smiled, nodded. He slapped the kid on the shoulder, handed over the rifle. The kid popped off three rounds.

"Yes!" he said.

He walked back to the car and got in.

"Thank you, Sir," he said.

"You want to give this man a ride?" Horses asked.

"Hell no."

They waved and drove away, Hubbard standing in the road holding the rifle above his head like some warrior Apache. They honked. It sounded like a sad goose.

Then Hubbard passed out.

HORSES COLLECTED HIS RIFLE and racked it. He started up the truck. He punched his Redbone tape out of the deck and rummaged in his box of music. He didn't like the Carlos Nakai stuff—tweedly flutes. He liked guitars. He found Led Zep II. He smiled, slotted it, fired up another cancer stick, and put the truck in gear. Hubbard was back there flat on the blacktop as fried eggs on a griddle. Splayed was the word Horses was looking for.

He rolled on down the lonesome highway.

Twenty feet south, he hit his brakes.

"Damn it," he said.

He slammed it in Park and got out and trotted back to Hubbard. He scooped him up and brought him to the truck in a fireman's carry. He opened the back door of the long cab, held it open with one toe, and tossed Hubbard on the seat. He went back to the Volvo and used his belt knife to unscrew the license plates. He dug the paperwork out of the glove compartment, snagged the duffel. He tossed them in with the snoring white man and slammed the doors and drove away.

He had hours to go. He'd be at the party late, but he'd make it. Hell, the party'd go on all night anyway. He whistled along with Plant and Page. He thought about Hubbard committing felony car assassination and laughed out loud. Wait till the Oyate guys found this guy passed out in the back seat! They'd think up all kinds of evil shit to do to him.

It was a good day: ten miles ahead, on the port side of the highway, Horses knew of a buffalo herd he liked to watch. And beyond that, to starboard, a llama ranch that had recently added ostriches. It was like a free trip to the zoo. Ostriches in Wyoming. And the Rockies would appear out of the blue haze, and the sun would shoot spears of light from between the peaks as it set. A fat orange moon would illuminate the world like a blacklight.

Horses had plans. He remembered the time he and Brewer duct-taped Ralph Morning Spider to the ceiling when he passed out drunk at a party in Porcupine. Morning Spider looked like he was flying when he woke up and started kicking and swinging his arms. Horses laughed again.

Those Oyate boys, a hundred years ago, they might have set Hubbard on fire, maybe staked him out on an ant hill. But duct tape! That was funny. Hubbard would open his eyes and see crazy Indians dancing beneath him in a cloud of smoke and noise. Arms wide against the ceiling, unable to come down. Eyes like plates.

Hubbard, caught up in the sky.

Hubbard, learning to pray.

FIRST LIGHT

I want to do with you
what spring does with the cherry trees.
—Neruda

THE TRES ESTRELLAS BUS coughed once and spat out a blue
puff of exhaust. Its brake lights flared, and it lumbered away, all
eighteen wheels crushing sea shells and wadded knots of newspaper. I listened to the engine chew through the gears, then the bus
was gone. The street stood deserted.

Muted trumpet bleats echoed in the distance, then dogs, then
crickets. I couldn't see my uncle's white Ford anywhere, so I started into
the terminal, glancing at the bullfight and lucha libre posters (Mil
Máscaras vs. El Piloto Atómico!). Some strands of Christmas lights
still clung to the light posts, but apparently only the red bulbs were
working.

Inside, behind a tin counter encrusted with beer decals, a
fabulously ugly man stirred fruit juice in a big clear plastic jug with
its top cut off. Slumbering on folding chairs, old women like
bundles of sticks wrapped in black cloth. Sleepy eyed boys offering
trays of chewing gum. I leaned on the counter and gestured toward
the agua de piña. He nodded and pushed a dipper through the slabs
of ice and said, "Pie scent."

Pie scent? I thought, staring blankly.

"You money—pie scent," he repeated.

Oh! I thought.

"Cinco centavos?" I said.

He squinted one eye at me.

"You no gringo cabrón?" he asked.

"Born in Mexico," I shrugged.

"Ah caray!" He slapped the bar once and roared. "Más Mexicano que las tortillas," he said. He dipped me up another cup of pineapple juice. He laughed so hard the juice slopped all over. I snatched the tall paper cup out from under the cascade. He was laughing because the joke was on him. I offered him a palmful of coins, but he waved me away.

"Gringo cabrón," he sighed, wiping his eyes.

Outside, I could see some little black thing swimming in my cup. I fished it out and flicked it into the dark, then sat on the high curb, thinking about the Ford and feeling nervous. I gulped the cold juice. I caught myself posing in case she were with them. I rested my chin on my fist—the lost poet. I leaned back, feet splayed on the cobbles—Jim Morrison. Head hung down, hands dangling between my knees—the weary traveler. What would she think? How would she feel, seeing me again? I knew how I'd feel. I was working without a net.

I could still see her, as though she were there before me. It had been two years since I had last entered their house, been pummeled and hugged by uncle, aunt, cousin after cousin, all the time searching frantically through my smile. Then seeing the door to the back room open a crack, and one eye watching me, and my legs wobbled a little, my breath slipping as she stepped out and her lips sent a crackling bolt into my gut. Her eyes ate me up and she whispered "Henry" in my ear as we hugged and my dry mouth managed to say, "Cristina."

I tossed my empty cup onto the cobbles.

It was too far into the city for the sea breeze to reach.

Mazatlán had its backstreet smell, the tang of seaweed and spoiled fruit, sharp as the sweat of the streets. The backs of my knees felt greasy, and I was watching a black dog click down the road when I heard a horn tap out a rapid tattoo, the Mexican code that suggested I do something rude to my mother. I started laughing, poses forgotten, as the big car crunched slowly to my toes and stood, grumbling. My cousins Panchito and Marcos grinned at me. She wasn't there.

Panchito sprung from the car with his usual energy and grace. Marcos the Bull sneered at me, his hair greased back and sparkling, his lip curling over a gold-edged tooth. Panchito lifted me off the ground as we embraced and traded the usual insults.

"Any news of the Beatles?" he asked.

"I'm fine, thanks," I replied.

I lifted a finger, turned to my suitcase. Much cryptic clicking and fiddling, and I lifted the White Album over my shoulder, never looking back at him. I could hear his breath suck in. I had his sister; he had the Beatles.

"Two disks," I intoned.

He snatched it, cackling, and photos of John Paul Jorge y Ringo scattered out of the sleeve. They slithered across the sidewalk, and I turned to pick them up, and the Bull stood there, fists on hips, eyeing me coolly.

"The Beatles are faggots," he said.

I shrugged.

He looked at my boots and laughed: "Heh heh heh."

I wanted to pry his mouth open and force him to say Ha.

Panchito had this way of whistling while trilling his lips, perfectly duplicating a cricket's chirp. He was busy with my bags, going "prree-ppree-prree." The Bull said, "Did you ever, heh-heh-heh, learn to box?"

When I was little, he'd punched me silly.

"No."

He threw his hands up and bobbed his head.

"Might have to teach you all over again," he said.

Panchito and I looked at each other. I pushed past the Bull and got in the car. He raised his head, belched once, and followed.

WE SLICED THROUGH the heavy night, engine humming. Panchito wanted to know what the words "glass onion" meant. Marcos glanced at me, slumped in the passenger seat.

"You're awfully quiet, little cousin," he leered.

Everything he said sounded dirty.

"I've been on a bus for thirty hours," I said.

"It was worth it. Better than hanging around the pinche border."

"Wait until you see the theater!" Panchito cried from the back.

"Movies," the Bull said.

"Expanding your empire?" I asked him.

"Well, well," he grumbled. "Aren't we revolutionary."

After a moment, I said, "Forgive me. I'm tired."

He blew air through his nose.

"The only movie theater in one hundred kilometers," he said. "And how's the family?"

He nodded.

"Cristina?"

"Son of a whore," the Bull said, matter-of-factly. "It took you twenty-two minutes."

Stupidly, I glanced at my watch.

"She's my cousin," I protested lamely. "What's wrong with asking?"

"Exactly," said the Bull. "She's your cousin."

Panchito poked me in the back with one finger. He asked brightly, "Any women on that bus?"

The Bull grinned—he couldn't help himself.

Thank you, Panchito, I thought, saying, "Yeah, sure."

The Bull lit a Domino cigarette.

"The stewardess," I continued.

"On a bus?" he snorted.

"It's true!" Panchito said. "I've seen it."

"Lies."

"Oh really?" I grinned, pulling a scrap of paper from my pocket.

"Let me see that!" the Bull demanded, grabbing for it. I pulled it out of his reach and Panchito snagged it. He whistled. "Come on! Come on!" the Bull snapped.

"It's her address and phone number," Panchito said, handing it over to Marcos. "Henry, you dog."

Marcos cursed.

"Big tits?" he asked.

"Like little limes."

He was wearing me out.

"Who needs little tits?" he asked.

He wadded the paper and opened his window.

"Hey!" I said.

He tossed it out.

"Bitches with no tits aren't women at all." His talking made the red end of his cigarette dance crazily.

A burro zipped by my window like a tatter of fog. I drummed my fingers.

"Look," I said. "She was nice. She was a fine person. All woman."

"That's nice," the Bull said. "Really nice. But don't let me catch you playing your little tricks on my sister."

The lights of the town were showing at the base of the mountains.

"Prree-prree-prree," Panchito suggested.

THE HOUSE SEEMED ABLAZE and an immense clatter poured into the street as García-García, my uncle, pounded my back and poked me in the belly, bellowing, "Too many tortillas for you, Henry! Too many tortillas!" My aunt called me an angel (*Where is*

Cristina?) and said, "You're too skinny." (*Any second she'll come out.
Any second now.*) Antonio, the oldest cousin, and his wife Flora
embraced me. Panchito turned on the stereo and threw the needle
down with a Boom! on an accordion-driven rave-up that screamed:
"¡Ya llegó el que estaba ausente!"

América, my littlest cousin, twisted her skirt around her chubby
fingers, asking my aunt, "Who is that?" then being forced to plant
one of those wet popping little girl kisses on my cheek, then her
sister Gabriela was there, Panchito goosing me, announcing, "I am
duh Waldrress," Marcos dancing with América, the thin dark faces
of poor folk peering in through the iron bars on the windows as if
these rich bastards were in a zoo, and a parrot shouted hysterically
from a big white cage in the corner when a cool hand touched my
arm and the world cut to slow-motion and I faced her. Shining lips.
Saying: "Cousin."

Uncle García wrestled with a case of beer. She glanced quickly
at him. She licked her lips. I thought: Yum Yum! She smiled.

"And how was your trip? Not too exhausting, I trust?"

"Cristina," I said, going to embrace her. The slightest of head-
shakes. I was stupid, I was heroic. I shook her hand. "I'd have
walked," I said.

"Just to see a movie?" she replied.

"I'd do many things," I announced, "for a movie."

"Grand opening soon!" Panchito said.

She let go of my hand—I realized I'd been clutching it. Later,
my fingers would smell like her. She turned and drifted through the
room like a white feather, parting the chaos.

"Food!" García shouted.

"Beer!" the Bull proclaimed.

Green lizards scurried over the walls and tap-danced across the
ceiling. Las cachoras. And I was looking up at them, thinking how I
had missed them, their quiet chirps, and it seemed as though in that
instant I was in my bed in the back room off the courtyard, all of
them snoring upstairs, and her smell on my palm. Startled by the

silence. I could have slept through the Coronas and Dos Equis bottles, the toasts, her sly looks, the meal, the mangos. The ordering of the girls to bed, their legs rising, her legs going up, going up, knees dimpling as she climbed. García breaking out the brandy, raising a snifter and intoning a great lecture about cinema, the revolution in thinking about to hit the town, more money in the coffers! Laughter. Then he rose with my aunt, and Antonio and Flora left, and Marcos staggered off to bed, and Panchito and I were left downstairs, huddled over the stereo, where he seemed to breathe in the Beatles' melodies like air. "Qué es Rocky Raccoon?" And the cachoras sang from behind the paintings on the walls.

When the tone arm lifted off the last song and the machine clicked off, he put his hand on my knee and said, "You love her."

"It's our secret."

"It's a beautiful secret."

He smiled. His face was sweet and sad. He hugged me once and said, "Good night, my brother."

Now I was alone. Their sleeping rooms had all been moved upstairs in the last two years, and I had the entire ground floor to myself. The room was in the back, far away from them, and it had a small bathroom. The little courtyard was overrun with vines. A tattered banana tree. A spider the size of a dinner plate clutched the wall above my bed and seemed to ponder my face.

I switched off the light. I was seeing her in the black above my room. The X-Ray Vision of Love. Mosquitoes vectored in like minuscule fighter jets. A really intelligent rooster crowed at the moon. The ache of exhaustion carried me like warm water, and I was going with it, going toward the horizon, when I heard my door open. I sat up, trying to blink away the dark. A pale shape was there.

I could smell her. Tears rolled out of my eyes, hot enough to glow. I was always reduced to nothing before her. There was no defense.

"Are you awake?" she whispered.

"I love you."

"Oh," she said. "Talking in your sleep?"

"I can hear you smiling."

"I'm crying, Henry. Isn't that silly?"

"Ridiculous," I said, wiping my eyes on the sheet.

We hung there, droplets shaking on the edge of a leaf. We giggled, and she moved. Looking like a cloud in the night, she came to stand beside my bed. I reached out to find her belly. It was warm and tender through the cotton of her gown. I pulled her down. We held each other hard. I wanted our ribs to intertwine.

"Why, Daddy!" she whispered, as though we'd been discovered. "It's not what you think! We're just wrestling!" She laughed into my shoulder.

"Yeah, Tío! We bet five pesos. I take on Marcos next."

We laughed too hard. She pulled my pillow out from under my head to cover her mouth but my head smacked the wall and we laughed harder. I had to bite the mattress. The terror was delicious.

"If they find us," she gasped.

"We'll be dead."

"Our troubles will be over."

I put my fingers over her mouth. She covered my palm and kissed my hand. My heart was trying to outrun hers.

"I must go," she said.

She slipped through my hands.

Pausing at the door, she said the strangest thing, a thing that seemed crazy at the time. She said, "Promise me one thing, Henry. Vow to me one thing."

"Anything," I said.

"Don't give me an easy answer. Mean it."

"I mean it."

"Promise me that no matter what happens to either of us, you will never hate me, or forsake me. Or…" she breathed, "be like the rest of them."

I started to answer her, but she said, "Shhh." Then she was gone.

I baked all night in the heat of her scent.

THE BASKETBALL bounced off my head, shattering my sleep.

"What? What?"

Panchito grinned at me in the gloomy light.

"What time is it?" I mumbled.

"Before six," he chirped.

I pulled the sheet over my head, moaning. He tugged at it. I was growling like a dog by then, and Panchito was shuffling back and forth, holding the edge of the sheet in his teeth. We formed a crazed pendulum.

"Basketball," he snarled around a mouthful of percale.

"No."

"You and me and the boys."

"No."

"You'll feel great."

"Don't want to feel great."

"You'll get in shape."

"I'd rather die."

He stood, bouncing the ball. It went *blount-blount-blount* on the cement floor.

"Have a good game," I suggested from under my pillow.

"Cristina needs someone to accompany her to the market," he yawned.

I erupted from the bed in a billow of sheets and charged for the shower, unhooking my underpants with one thumb as I went.

"Bravo!" he called. "Bravísimo!"

THE WALLS OF THE TOWN looked like thick coats of icing had smeared each house together. Creamy colors went into each other, and the only way to tell where one house ended and another began was the glaring border between the bright yellow and the harsh blue. It was often a green or red drainpipe. Roosters and burros were berserking all over town. Dawn was the only time of day that offered up a fresh, cool breeze. Clouds scudded from the hills, the cobbles looked like small loaves of bread in the street, birds chittered along the sky like hot coals skipping across a puddle. The blue milkpot pinged against my leg. Cristina walked fast, hair glorious, wild. Ten paces behind, the grumpy América and Gabriela followed, rubbing their eyes, spying.

I smelled the market before we got there. It smelled sweet and foul, the scent of fruit and just-slaughtered meat, coffee and rot, honey and mud. We turned the corner and I was assaulted by the grannies in black, bumping through the crowd and haggling over leaky disks of goat cheese. Fat bees bounced off the rows of glistening candied fruits. I was bopping, rocking on the balls of my feet, engaging in some foolish domestic daydream.

While we tarried over the displays of food, I crooned to her in a bogus lounge-lizard voice. Since she'd never been in a cocktail lounge, had never heard a lounge-lizard, the singing had a fascinating effect. I unleashed an "Oh yeah, bay-buh!" The little sisters shook their heads in disgust. They wandered away.

"I have a Christmas present for you-oo," I sang.

"And I've got one for you too-oo," she replied.

"What?" I demanded.

She shook her head and walked away. I watched her bottom move under her skirt. I felt all-powerful. I went searching for the little monsters.

I found them ogling a case packed with membrillo, bisnaga, camote and dulce de leche candies.

"I have a vast sum of money," I announced, "with which to purchase a great pile of candy."

They watched me.

"This treasure is to go directly into your stomachs."

Gabriela started to smile, but caught herself just in time and managed a scowl.

"I don't like the look of these," I said. The girls peered into the case.

"These are full of fly eggs. The worms will come out your noses." They pulled faces. I waved a bill before Gabriela's face. She snatched it and they scurried off, looking for a better candy case.

"What a brilliant man," I said as I walked back to Cristina's side.

"Who?"

"Me. I got rid of the girls."

She pointed across the way. There, between a double pyramid of pineapples, their four beady eyes glared at me. Wicked beasts. Discolored goop was upon their mouths like blood.

I think I barked.

Whatever noise I made, she leaned back and laughed. "You're really something," she said.

"I am remarkable," I agreed.

"Humble, too."

She squeezed an avocado. Her nails were pink against the deep green. When she said, "I'm going down to Doña Petra's stall to buy some milk," it was the greatest thing I'd ever heard.

"Milk?" I cried. "Yes! Let's go buy some!"

Doña Petra was four feet tall, three feet wide, and had a hairy wart beside her nose. I loved her.

"Cristina, dear," she crowed while pouring thin blue milk through a cheesecloth. "Who is this big boy?"

"My cousin Henry, Señora."

"Oh my!" Doña Petra cawed. "Your cousin Henry! Of course! He's as handsome as your father!"

I started to reply with some self-effacing thing that might impress Cristina with its gallantry when Doña Petra's steel rail arm swept me away from Cristina's side. The old voice croaked into my ribs: "Come see my daughter! You'll love my daughter. Nina! Nina, come see Henry, he's handsome like his uncle!" I was trying to look back at Cristina, but Petra had caught me like a whirlpool. I was spun around to face Nina. She was all of fourteen, skinny, in a frenzy of blushing. She stared intently at her curd-encrusted shoes. She was a neon sign of embarrassment: blink blink blink.

"Nina, isn't he a *big* boy?"

Blink.

"Say hello to Nina."

"Hello, Nina."

Blink blink.

"Tell her how pretty she is."

"Nina, you are so pretty I forget to breathe."

Blink blink blink blink.

Petra smashed me one on the back so hard I coughed. I staggered out to the street and heard her Har Har booming all through the market.

Cristina waited outside (pot hanging from her left hand, right arm crossed over her abdomen, pushing up her breasts, right hand on left elbow, skin like fire in the sunrise).

"Are you through flirting?" she asked.

"I think I need a doctor," craning up to rub my back.

América whined beside her.

"I don't feel good," she said.

Gabriela was looking fairly puce also. I was feeling a certain glee at finding no candy in their hands.

"You ate too much, didn't you?" Cristina snapped. Her ferocity startled even me. "What a pair of little pigs!"

América's lower lip disengaged itself from the copious residue on her face and hung out, trembling.

Cristina shoved the pot at them and said, "You take this milk home now! And wash your faces!" She clapped her hands once, like thunder. The girls broke and ran.

She turned to me smiling and said, "Freedom."

"You're a genius."

"I'm a woman."

"WHY THE CEMETERY?" I asked as we went through the splintery gate. The graveyard stood between the town and the highway, that old two-lane blacktop that ran west to the sea, then cut north, into the deserts.

"It's quiet," she said. "Besides, wherever we go, people are watching us. At least these people will never tell."

The graves had cement caps over them, like small faux marble tombs with cracked corners. She sat on one of the graves. Tarantulas felt their ways between the stones, seeking shelter from the coming heat. Cristina played with the dry weeds. Blew on the white and puffy head of a dandelion. The thistles spun like a hundred little helicopters, and the wind pushed them into her breasts.

"I want to make love to you," I blurted.

"Oh, that." She didn't even look up at me. "Is that what you want?" She looked at her hands. They were long, slender, strong. "Sex. I think that's the thing that matters least."

She was about to say more. She had a look on her face—but then the car was suddenly there in a billow of dust. Marcos raced the engine and opened the door.

"Get your ass home and cook breakfast!" he shouted.

It took her so long to get up that she seemed to turn into an old woman. I watched her walk past the car, brush its hood lightly with her fingertips.

"Get in," he said.

He was full of nasty joy, manly fun. We sped, scattering chickens. He made endless jokes which I didn't really hear. I just laughed at appropriate moments like a machine programed for hilarity. We picked up Panchito and drove fast in no particular direction for no particular reason. Panchito was like a light in a coffin.

When we got to the breakfast table, García was expounding.

"Poor!" he shouted. "I'll tell you how poor they are! They have houses made of bricks!"

"Bricks," echoed Marcos.

"They want us to feel sorry for them in brick houses."

García gulped his coffee.

I sat down across from Cristina's empty seat and kicked off my huaraches. The family didn't approve of bare feet—bareness being a sure sign of poverty. I could only enjoy the cool floor when my feet were hid under the table. I couldn't see far enough into the kitchen to spy her, but I could hear the musical clatter of plates and pots.

Then she came in, placed a plate before her father, and a second plate before me. Two eggs fried perfectly, floating on a pond of salsa on a corn tortilla, staring up at me like eyes.

"Thank you," I said.

None of them said anything as she served them.

When she got to Panchito, he grabbed her and kissed her. "Who is the prettiest woman in Mexico? Hmm? It's you, isn't it? Yes, I think it's you." She slapped at him to get away. They were laughing.

Marcos said, "Are you going to serve me today, or what?"

She looked at him, not with anger, but with a terrible laxness. No feeling at all. "How shall I make your eggs?" she asked. In crude Spanish, this can also be taken to mean, How should I handle your balls? The Bull made his heh-heh-heh sounds and held up his palm and squeezed the air three or four times.

"Like this would be nice," he said.

"Fine," Cristina said into his ear. "Go cook your own."

Marcos goggled as she sat down to her already-cold food. Panchito snorted into his glass of milk, sending it out through his nose. García rattled his morning paper—all two pages of it. My aunt glared at her, then at me. Cristina's face remained composed, but I could see it—she was smiling behind her lips. My aunt said, "Don't fret yourself, my angel," patting the Bull's hand. "I'll make it for you."

"Bricks," García said. "Beggars in brick houses."

"If they build on our land," Marcos declared, "I'll take your pistol and show them who's boss."

Les enseño quien manda aquí.

García laughed.

Cristina didn't look at me.

I felt her toes tentatively touch mine under the table. Life looked better.

"They whine about not having food to eat," García continued, "but they can afford bricks. This is what I'm saying."

She pulled at the hair on my ankles. We were touching, we were slipping cool skin along each other's flesh, and it was right under their noses.

"Let them eat shit!" the Bull said.

"Now son," my aunt scolded, putting his plate before him.

I was overjoyed by his stupidity. The nose hairs García was plucking were quite nice at that point. I suggested that we all sing Christmas carols. Panchito backed me up with a prree-prree. We burst into a heavily accented version of "Bungalow Bill." Cristina smiled at her plate. I watched her make swirls of yolk with a triangle of tortilla, and her feet were telling me incredible things. The others drifted away from the table.

Panchito and I ate everything in sight and her skin was hitting me like wind that could blow me over the mountains.

WE FINISHED TYING the big speakers onto the roof of the Ford, running the ropes through the windows. Panchito looked at the list of announcements García had given him. He blew into the microphone; it sounded like a tornado.

"My life in advertising," I said.

"Do they do this in California?" he asked.

"You'd get arrested for disturbing the peace."

He thought for a moment, and said, "We don't have any peace." He looked again at the list typed on onionskin. "Guess what films we're offering tonight for the 'grand opening'."

I shrugged.

"John Wayne in *The War Wagon*."

"And?"

"*King Kong vs. Godzilla*."

"Maybe the winner has to fight John Wayne," I said.

We got into the car and Panchito bellowed into the mike: "Tamales! Get your fresh tamales here!"

I took it away from him and announced, "Tonight, in Cine García, filthy pornography! Banned by the Pope!"

Pancho: "Nude women!"

Me: "Motorcycles!"

Pancho: "Twelve altar boys!"

Me: "An elephant!"

García charged out the door sputtering as we drove away.

"See Godzilla, the primordial terror, eat John Wayne's head!"

A block from the house, on the road that curved right past the cemetery, Panchito spied a drunk sleeping in the shadow of the Banco de Comercio. "Hey! You!" he called. The poor fellow's feet were running before he was even up.

"I love this stinking town," he said. "That's why I hate it."

I nodded.

"Pancho," I replied, "that makes about as much sense as anything else around here."

He handed me the microphone.

"Don't panic," I declared. "Stay in your homes. Giant man-eating crickets have been spotted by the river." Pancho's eyes began to glimmer. "These crickets are the size of lions! Do not panic!" I held the mike to his lips. He went prree-prree-prree, and it was loud enough to rattle window glass. "These are Soviet crickets!/Prree!/ The same abominations/Prree/that devastated Cuba!/Prree!"

We were coming around a corner when he grabbed the mike from me.

"LOOK AT THOSE DOGS!" he shrieked.

"What dogs?"

"That's disgusting!"

"What dogs?"

"Ladies and Gentlemen, this is bad."

"I don't see any dogs."

"I am saddened, my people." Faces were appearing in the windows around us. We were at a dead stop in the middle of the street. "But it is obvious that someone has tied these dogs together. And the nice boy dog is trying to push the tired girl dog down the street! He's pushing. Pushing her! Unh! Unh! And...no, wait. Wait a minute, folks...."

"Uh," I said.

"Oh my God!"

"Stop."

"Filthy beasts!"

"I think we should drive away."

"Is there a priest present? We must marry these dogs immediately. Think of the children!"

People were coming out, looking for the dogs.

"Let's go," I said.

Clang! We spun around in our seats. Doña Petra had appeared, as if by magic, wielding a broom. She wound up for another swing. Nina could be seen on the curb, overcome with emotion. I waved at her inanely.

"Bad boys!" cried Doña P.

Clang!

"She really gets around," I said.

"Help!" Pancho shouted into the mike. "Rabid grandmothers have invaded Mexico!" *Bong!* "We are under attack!"

"Bad boys."

"Pancho, I think we should take a little drive. What do you think?"

Ping!

"Bad dirty boys."

As we drove away, I saw Doña Petra swing her attention on the louts on the corner, who were still laughing. She took a mighty swing at them, and they danced and skipped out of range. A samurai-like slash of the broom scattered them into the street.

"Shee," Panchito sighed, "this advertising work really tires me out."

"Me too."

"Time for a break," he said. He pulled up in front of the Cantina La Iguanita Verde. "I am dehydrated. The only remedy is beer."

By the time we got home, it was time for lunch. Carmela the

cook was on duty by then. Cristina was free to sit, never looking at me, while we fought like hard lovers with our toes. The little sisters watched every move. Carmela served bowls of fideo with banana slices floating in the clear broth. Rice fried in tomato and onion, beef sliced in paper-thin bistek portions and marinated in beer, beans, Coca Cola. Carmela conjured stacks of limp steamy tortillas.

My aunt whispered, "Be sure to put your things away carefully when she"—she gestured toward the kitchen—"is on duty. She steals."

"Oh come on."

"She steals from the rooms and stuffs it in her panties. You know how they are."

"Who?"

"Them. The dark ones. Come on, Henry—no seas simple. The indios."

I looked up. Carmela stood in the doorway, listening. I felt dirty for sitting there, letting her feed me while they insulted her. I shrugged at her, surreptitiously put my finger to the side of my head and screwed it around a couple of times. She smiled. She looked at the back of my aunt's head and sighed. She shrugged back at me and brought more tortillas.

As she leaned around Marcos, he sniffed.

"What's the smell?" he said.

He and García giggled.

Marcos picked up a yellow chile and poked it in her face. She flinched.

"Oh," he said, "am I molesting you with my chile?"

This, of course, also meant, May I rape you with my penis? He guffawed.

"He's a genius, isn't he?" I said. "A real poet. So much education reflected in his beautiful way of speaking."

Carmela laughed and hurried back to the kitchen.

Cristina was slowly stroking the top of my foot. I ran my toes up her calf, circled her knee. She squirmed.

García dropped his paper on the floor and said, "It's time for a siesta. Mother?" He held out his hand and my aunt took it and they went up to their hammocks. When they got to the top of the stairs, he called back down, "Julio called."

Cristina's face paled.

Marcos smiled.

"Who?" I asked.

Panchito pushed away from the table.

"He'll be here for the opening," García shouted.

"Who's Julio?"

"I'm gone," Panchito said. Cristina gathered her plates and went to the kitchen. I heard the front door slam and the car start up.

"Julio?"

The Bull lit a cigarette.

"Hey, culero," he said. "Who's Julio? Who's Julio?" He blew smoke at me. "Julio is Cristina's fiancé."

He formed a pistol with his fingers, laughed his weird triple laugh, and fired.

FIANCÉ? FIANCÉ.

I walked around the silent lower floor. Well, okay, I didn't own her. Yes I did. Why didn't she tell me? Hey, dude—relax. It'll be all right. It will never be all right.

I could hear García creaking in his hammock. My aunt was snoring.

Julio, eh?

I was sitting on my bed when she entered. She held a white bundle in her hands. Her eyes were wide with fear.

"Do you understand?" she said. "Do you?"

I said nothing.

She sat down beside me. I didn't move. I didn't want to touch her.

"Julio," she said. "He has a car, a house. He's studying at the university to be a professor."

"So am I," I whined.

Her hands twisted the fabric.

"Yes, but Julio isn't my cousin."

It felt like a kick.

"He lives in a city. Can't you understand?"

"Escape," I said.

"Yes!" A tear came down her cheek. "Away from here!"

"You don't need a man to escape."

"Henry, please. This isn't California."

I stared at the floor.

"Do you love him?" I asked.

She sighed.

We sat there.

I grabbed her hand.

"To hell with Julio," I said. "Come with me."

"Don't be stupid."

She pulled her hand away.

"Cristina...."

"No, Henry, no. No more. Please."

"Your handwriting makes me cry. I smell you on my hand and I can't sleep."

"It's not as simple as you think."

"But I love you!"

Her eyes flared.

"Love! You love me! Does that make you the special one? What about me!" She punched the bed. "Henry? What about me?" She looked into my eyes, back and forth, from eye to eye. "I do love you."

The house ticked like a forgotten clock.

"Feliz Navidad," she finally said, handing me the package. It was soft cotton. "Unfold it."

I did. A hand-sewn white shirt blossomed in my lap. It had an open throat and wooden buttons. Bluebirds in flight were painstakingly embroidered on the left breast. I ran my fingers over the smooth blue threads.

"I made it myself. I had to guess your size...do you like it?"

I put my hand on her waist and nodded.

"I spread it on my bed at night," she said. "And I sleep on it so it will smell like me."

I held it to my face. Her eyebrows went up. I nodded.

"Your smell," I said, "instead of you."

"It's all I have."

I went to my suitcase and dug through my jockey shorts and shirts. I found the hard little bundle. I handed it to her, and she untied the string and tore the paper and the small book fell into her lap. Neruda's *Twenty Love Poems and a Song of Despair*.

She said, "Poetry!"

She settled back and put her feet in my lap.

"Read me one," she said. "I've never had anyone read me a poem."

It was a slow death reading to her. It was an infinite ache.

I WALKED TO THE RIVER, head down. Escape, I told myself. Escape. And the most altruistic part of me said, Yes, of course. I understood, I honestly did. The rational part of me recognized the impossibility of our situation. Yet I had been waiting for her. I had been *saving myself* like some heroine in a bad romance book for her. Julio? I was resolved—my body demanded her. I would be with her first. That much would always be mine. Ours.

At the water's edge, I looked around. A blond woman knelt on the shore, working some bedsheets on the rocks. I watched the soap foam whip away on the current, and I thought, *That's the only blond hair I've seen since I came here.*

"Hello, Baby!" she called. Just like that. In English.

"Do you speak English?" I asked.

"Are you kidding? No." She looked me up and down. "You're new."

"I feel old."

"Don't we all." She laughed. "New in town?"

"Visiting."

"You're lucky."

I went to her side.

"Lucky to be here, huh?" I said.

"Lucky to only be visiting."

I caught myself looking down her blouse. She knew it, but she didn't change position. Panchito's voice came from town, distorted and reverberating: "See John Wayne grow to one kilometer in height! See the radioactive cowboy destroy Japan!"

She laughed.

"Está loco," she said.

"That's my cousin, Panchito," I said.

She snapped her fingers.

"García's nephew! I've heard about you." She held out her arm. "Help me up."

Her brown skin was hot. I felt the small muscle in her upper arm. The moistness of her sweat.

She held a dripping knot of sheets out to me and said, "Twist."

I grabbed hold and pulled back as we twisted, water pattering on the stones.

"I'm Henry," I said.

"Guadalupe," she nodded. "You know, your uncle wouldn't like it, you out here with me."

"Why not?"

She pushed hair out of her face with one wrist. Took the sheets back from me. "Boy," she said, "you really are new around here."

The car appeared from between two houses about fifty feet up the bank. Panchito broadcast: "Thank you, Ladies and Gentlemen, for tuning in to my show. El show de Pancho García. We play all the hits. Your sentimental favorites." His voice echoed up and down the river. "I would like to thank my special guest, Cousin Henry. He is currently working for the KGB as an assassin, and he will be back tomorrow with his favorite poison cooking tips."

A terrible roar resolved itself into "Revolution Number 9."

"He got a tape recorder!" I said.

But she was gone. I looked and saw her walking down the bank, hurrying along with her bundle of washing on top of her head. I watched as she turned into town and vanished.

"Nomberr Nine, Nomberr Nine," Panchito said. "Nomberr Nine."

I got into the car and switched off the little tape recorder.

"You knew."

"Knew what?"

"You bastard. You knew about Julio."

"Of course I knew."

"Why didn't you tell me?"

"Why didn't you ask?"

"Asshole!"

"Shit-head!"

We sat there, breathing hard.

"You met Blondie," he said. He put the car in gear and backed up.

"Guadalupe."

"So that's her name."

"She's nice."

"Nice?"

"A nice girl. I helped her with her washing."

"Nice! She's a whore. She works in the whorehouse."

"No."

"Yes."

"Oh no."

"Yes, yes. We've all had her."

"Julio?"

"Hell yes, Julio. She's blond, man. Everybody wants her."

I rubbed my face.

"Nice," he said. "You're so naive."

He drove along; I sulked. He pulled over. He leaned back in his seat, stiff-armed the wheel. "Let me tell you a story," he said. "Papá decided long ago to educate his children, no? All of us, Antonio, the Bull, me, Cristi, we all went to high school. Then, one by one, we boys went to university. All the time, Papá was promising her a chance, too. She wanted to be a doctor. So she watched her friends get older and stupider. The girls all started to marry. And then Papá decided it wasn't worth the money to send the girls to college. Do you see? She was on the verge. All the world was about to open to her. She'd never even left this town! She was about to join us in the city…and then they told her no." He shook his head. "Papá told her to face it—she'd only end up marrying somebody, making babies. Why be educated? He told her it would just make her miserable. Mother and Father told her they were being humane. They told her it was love."

He laughed without mirth.

"No more dreams, brother. No tomorrow."

I nodded.

"Escape," I said.

"I guess."

We drove into town.

A blue Plymouth stood before the theater.

"Julio," said Pancho.

WE STEPPED INTO the dark moviehouse. The dark was not cool. Two tall fans throbbed in the heat to no avail. García held court: "We have installed metal seats, gentlemen of the press," (my cousin Antonio was the only reporter in town, and he published the daily two-sheet,) "so that when certain rougher elements of our fair city become emotional, they might bend them, but not break them, as would be the case with older, wooden seats such as those in the Mazatlán baseball stadium." His hand swept up in a grand gesture. "Note too our modern air conditioning system." He gestured to the fans, then to the raised tin roof. Between it and the tops of the walls there were open triangles of air, through which fruit bats and little mud-dauber birds tumbled.

My eyes adjusted to the gloom and saw other bats hanging from the corrugations like brown fruit. The bats were going to love the movies. Bat piss and guano misting down on the viewers. My eyes went across the bat rookery and down the back wall. There they sat, in a far row, Cristina and Julio. They were leaning toward each other, speaking with some passion. She was waving her hands. He shook his head. She put her hand on her brow. He stood up. He was tall, sleepy-eyed and brutal. He looked sexy. He glanced at me, nodded once, and said something else to her. She stared at me. He grabbed her hand and pulled her my way.

"Henry," he said, his voice deep and somehow pushed down into his chest. "My next cousin." He gave me an abrazo, slapping me on the back. He smelled tangy. He moved on to Panchito, saying, "And you, cabrón," and they made a lot of noise. She stood watching him, a certain light in her eyes that made me mad.

"I thought you didn't love him," I said.

"Well, I *like* him," she said.

"Good God!" García yelled. "I forgot to pick up the movies!"

Much scurrying. Julio grabbed my arm. He threw his arm around Cristina. She snagged Panchito. "I'll drive!" Julio boomed. García gasped in elaborate horror. Then we were out, and I was just floating on the pandemonium.

Pancho and I slid into the back seat. She sat sideways in the passenger seat, facing Julio. Julio hung a cigarette off his heavy lip. "What a family!" he said and we were off, tires screaking on the cobbles.

We were laughing at his foolish jokes. So was he—he knew they were foolish. Panchito looked at me as if to say, See? He's not so bad. The car skidded a bit, and Julio reached back to pat my knee as he drove with his left hand, bounced off a high curb. The hubcap made a sharp crack against the cement. Julio cried, "You're a good man, Henry!" And Pancho said, "He's a dog, there's no doubt about it." I was thinking Julio really wasn't that bad at all when Cristina said, "Watch where you're going."

"What?" he said.

"Don't drive so fast. You're being wild."

He slammed his foot on the brake, throwing her against the dashboard and the windshield. Her head knocked against the glass and she fell forward, off the seat.

"Collect yourself," he said.

She pulled herself up onto the seat.

"And don't you ever fucking tell me what to do or how to drive. Do you understand?"

She nodded.

"Do. You. Understand?"

"Yes." She smiled at him. "Mi amor."

Panchito put his hand on my arm and shook his head. I was trembling with rage.

"Go home," Julio said.

"All right," she replied.

She got out stiffly and closed the door. I watched her walk away. She never glanced at us.

"Women and dogs," Julio said. "A good one only needs to be beat two or three times." He laughed. He hit the gas. He said, "Right, boys? Right?"

His head looked huge in the deepening shadows.

THERE WAS QUITE A CROWD that night, filling the sidewalk and spilling into the street, blocking the old cars coughing out there. García stood tall and pompous, accepting handshakes and ignoring my aunt. I spotted Carmela slipping in the door with a gangly guy in a straw cowboy hat. She nodded to me once. In spite of the heat, I was wearing one of Pancho's blazers. He was up in the projection booth, drinking beer and learning how the machine worked. Julio found Cristina and said, "Sorry, baby." I was shocked when he was immediately forgiven and they walked in together.

"Sit by me," she said as they passed.

"Rich boy," muttered a tough boy on the street.

Marcos jumped down off the curb and sailed a punch past his chin, making him step back in a flinch.

He hopped up next to me and tapped me one on the jaw.

"Going to get drunk tonight, heh-heh-heh."

Big bats exited in a panic.

Inside, it was Julio on the aisle, then Cristina, then me. Rancheros hooted. Matches sputtered as they flew through the air. América and Gaby scooted around me and bounced into their seats, kicking their feet. Doña Petra went by and waggled her finger at me. Nina blinked and covered her mouth. Cristina turned and stared at me.

"Take off the jacket," she said. I let her tug the sleeve and pull it off. Julio had popcorn soaked in jalapeño juice. We were all drinking a local root beer made in a small plant by the river.

The lights dimmed. A beer bottle smashed against the screen. Whistles, shouts.

"Dumbshits," Julio said.

Scratchy sound, then theme music blasted out of the speakers. Applause. She leaned toward me in the dark, so our arms touched. Credits. "Keerk Dooglass!" Julio cried. John Wayne appeared onscreen. He was speaking German. A strip of Japanese subtitles flickered above a faded Spanish script. Kirk Douglas said, "Mach schnell!" Cristina crossed her arms, reaching under her elbow and laying fingers on my skin. Her fingers traced my arm for all four hours, plus cartoons. The Roadrunner had nothing on me. I was two separate John Waynes and several assorted Godzillas.

Like everything else between us, it was over too soon. The films ended and the lights came up and García collected his females and herded them along like a bull elk looking to do battle with any rogue male in sight. I found myself in the Plymouth with the muchachos, speeding around town, past the boneyard, howling. We drank from erupting bottles of beer. Pancho and Julio in front, the Bull and me in the rear. The Bull swigged from a bottle of tequila. His breath smelled like rot.

"Whores!" he shouted.

"Whores!" Julio concurred.

We rushed to the place, a cinderblock mass with "Men's Club" painted on the wall. Everyone piled out in drunken hilarity. What was Cristina doing at that moment? Brushing her hair? Undressing? Rubbing cream on her legs?

Panchito appeared before me and said, "This should be interesting." I followed him in.

WE WERE WATCHING a tiny guy in a Pemex shirt dance with one of the women. The two of them looked like the opposite ends of a horse somehow unconnected and kicking. A huge black velvet painting of the Virgin of Guadalupe hung over the bar. Votive candles burned before it.

Julio had found a baseball cap somewhere, and he had it scrunched down on his head. "Watch this," he said and wiggled his ears. The hat went forward and back on his head, forward and back.

Panchito was looking sentimental.

"I'm a sweet guy," he said. "I am basically a tender, loving man."

Marcos stared stupidly at a point on the wall for so long I thought he was asleep.

"I mean," Panchito confided, "I am sweet. Chingado! I'm sweet."

I stared at Julio, who busied himself with his cap-waggling and his bottle of Dos Equis. He'd never know, I thought. He'd never find out that Cristina and I had made first love with each other. Maybe tonight, when I got back to the house. Surely she'd be waiting for me. I smiled. I raised my beer to him.

"Salud," I said.

He made the cap wiggle.

Panchito said, "Blondie!"

"Hello, boys," Guadalupe said. "Looking for fun, I see."

"Guadalupe," I said.

She patted my arm.

"Good evening, gringo cousin," she said.

Julio turned in his chair and gaped up at her. "Henry!" he shouted.

Others turned to look at our table. "You know this whore?" He laughed, looked around at the muchachos. "You're already screwing the whores in this town?" He slapped the table. "I thought you were a queer!"

Before I could say anything, she leaned in close to his ear and said, very clearly, "You're the only whore I see in the whole place."

Julio's face went darker. He pulled his cap off his head and half-rose from his seat. Blondie raised one finger and the bartender stepped forward with a baseball bat in his hands.

"Stand up," she said.

Julio glanced at the bartender and stalled out, looking like he had to take a crap.

"Hell," Blondie sneered, "I might kick your ass myself."

He sat back down.

"Dance with me, Henry," she said.

I got up and stepped into her arms. Her smell was rich and sweet, alive with spice and tang and perfume and skin.

Panchito clapped.

"That was fun," I said.

"He's a pig."

Her back was hot.

"They're all pigs."

"I'm not a pig," I said.

"Not yet."

We dipped. I twirled her and reeled her in.

"Do you love me, Henry?"

"Sure."

"Above all others?"

"Oh yeah."

She lay her head on my shoulder.

"Liar."

The next song started and we danced some more.

"Are you going to buy me?"

"I don't think so."

"That's good," she said. "But you can pay me for the dance."

I said, "I thought you girls had hearts of gold."

She snorted. "Gold! Gold goes in the bank."

"I thought we were being romantic."

"Grow up."

The record ended. I went to kiss her. She turned her head.

I paid her.

She walked away.

The room was moving around me. I was weepy. Maudlin. I could save Guadalupe, I really could. I could take her home and we could live in a little bungalow and I could study for my finals while she cooked tamales.

Panchito rubbed my shoulders.

"You're a sweet man," he said. "Honest. There is a sweetness in the whole world!" We staggered out. Julio wanted to fight, but he fell over and puked. Marcos was draped over the hood of the car. "We're going to get some booze!" Pancho exulted.

"Not me," I said. "Take me home."

They called me a little girl and an old woman. They dropped me off and drove away singing. I managed to get the door open and locomoted across the floor and dove into bed. The humongus spider pattered up the wall. I swore I could hear its feet on the brick. I squinted at the clock, which was flying through the air in wild loops, and was astounded to see it was only 11:15. I pondered this until 11:30.

Then she came.

"I'VE GOT TO TALK to you," she said.

"Lie with me."

"Henry."

"Lie with me now. Then we can talk."

"Be serious."

"I am serious."

Silence.

"What?" I said. "You don't want me?"

She sat beside me. I reached out and touched her leg. She moved it away from me.

"What's wrong?"

She took a deep breath.

"Henry—do you remember your vow?"

I was trying to sober up fast.

"Yes, of course."

"Never to hate me."

"Yes."

"Never forsake me."

"Yes!"

The room had stopped spinning. Her nervousness was making me itchy.

"I don't want to marry him."

"Then don't!" I cried, joyously. "Come with me!" Hadn't I just thought this very thing in the whorehouse? *Grow up.*

"I can't," she choked.

"Mi vida, who cares? Who really cares if we're cousins? In California, nobody will even know—"

"Henry, will you please listen? I can't."

"I love you," I said.

She crossed her arms across her belly, leaned forward, and said, "I'm pregnant."

"Wha-hat?" I laughed.

"Julio got me pregnant, and it's going to show soon."

I couldn't breathe. He must have been laughing at me the whole time. And her. Her. Telling her all the time how much I loved her. Oh, Christ. *I want to make love to you.* I scooted back from her.

"No."

Visions of him digging in her.

"Please, talk to me."

"Go away."

"You're the only one who knows me."

"Get out of here."

"Don't you see?" she pleaded. "It doesn't matter what...what happened with him." She cried. "My heart will always be with you."

"Your heart."

"I know where you were tonight," she said. "I know what you were doing. *It doesn't matter.* Nothing can change what we feel."

She reached for me. She put her hand on my face. She opened her mouth, took another breath—I could feel she was about to say something else, something worse.

"I've only seen one whore tonight," I whispered.

How gray she went. How silent. She stared over my shoulder at the wall. Then she rose.

My arm was weak when I reached out, my fingers barely brushing her.

"I didn't mean it."

"Good night," she said.

Her feet slapped quietly through the dark of her home. I heard her rise, calling softly, "Papá, wake up. Papá! I have to talk with you."

"No," I said, and I raced out of the room, tripped on the stairs.

García shouted, "You're *what?*" The horrible dry slap of his palm rocked her as I stumbled up. She fell back against the wall, limp. She righted herself with one hand, smiled at us, and went in her room, swinging the door shut.

García stood in his stained underwear, panting, white in the face. His shorts sagged sadly between his defeated thighs, and I could hear my aunt weeping in her room. Cristina's room remained silent and dark. I went back down to the blackness of the bottom floor.

Lizards. Spiders.

THE BULL BURST THROUGH my door and slammed his fist into my head.

Blood spurted into my mouth. "Son of a whore!" he shouted. "I told you to keep your filthy"—he kicked me— "hands"—another kick—"off my sister!" He jammed his knee into my spine and pulled my head back by the hair. "I'll break your neck."

I heaved my back and bounced him off. I wasn't a little boy anymore. I blocked his next shot and landed two sharp lefts in his eye. He grabbed his face and fell back. I put my foot against his throat.

"It wasn't me."

Marcos threw a wild shot into my crotch. I hit the floor like a dropped shoe.

Panchito appeared on the Bull's back, riding him around the room, knocking things over. García was shouting from his room.

"Marcos! Marcos!" Pancho was shouting. "You idiot! Henry's only been here a couple of days! He couldn't have!"

"It was Julio," I gasped.

Marcos grabbed for me. I kicked him in the head to get my point across.

"Julio," I said.

Hell, he needed another whack, and I gave it to him. He developed an instant blood moustache.

"You didn't touch her?" he said.

I shook my head.

"You never touched her?"

"Of course not."

He got up.

"You stupid shit," he said. "You could have laid her in a second."

He fell out my door and vanished in the gloom.

I was going to say something to Panchito, but I passed out.

WHEN I AWOKE, there was a vague light in the sky. Panchito sat on the edge of the bed. "What a night," he said. I smiled, but my lips were split. I winced.

"Papá is announcing a big wedding today. It'll be in the paper." He leaned back against me. "You mind?"

"No."

"You're pretty comfortable," he noted.

"Don't make me laugh. It hurts."

"Let's go, Henry," he said.

"Where?"

"Go."

"Go?"

He held up the car keys.

"I mean, *go*."

"Steal the car?"

He nodded.

"Away?"

"I can't stay here anymore," he said. "It's driving me crazy."

"You're not serious."

"Do you want to stick around and watch her marry him?"

He had a point.

"But we can't just steal the car," I protested.

"Prree-prree," he argued.

He helped me to the shower. When the water was pouring, he said, "I had the girls pack our bags. Everybody else is still asleep after all the big excitement. They won't wake up for hours."

When I stepped out, I said, "Will she forgive me?"

He shrugged.

"Love forgives. Will you forgive yourself?"

I wanted to sing to her. I wanted to rub her living body. Read her more poems. I wanted to learn poetry and write sonnets to her.

"I'm miserable," Pancho said.

"Me too."

"I'm sorry."

"Me too."

I pulled on my pants. Cristina's shirt was on the bed. I dragged it on over my aching ribs. I breathed it in deep. A jade gecko chirped at me from the corner, did three push-ups. Panchito sighed.

"I'm leaving," he said.

"Yeah. Me too."

We lugged the bags out to the car. The speakers were still tied to the roof. We'd make a wonderful sight cutting through the deadly deserts of the north with our speakers rattling in the wind. It was a dim pearl color out there, but cool. Watermelon-scented wind blew in from the river, and there was a mockingbird somewhere scolding the sun. Panchito ran inside, and I sat in the car and fondled the cotton of the shirt. Her letter was tucked in the pocket.

> *My Henry,*
>
> *I dreamed of a lifetime of the taste of your mouth. I dreamed of a lifetime of our sleep together. I dreamed that your hand would lift me from the small hopes of my people.*
>
> *Did you dream of lifting me?*
>
> *Thank you for going. I couldn't get married with you there. Oh Henry, I will weep at the altar on that day, but not out of joy. And not for easy nostalgia. I will weep for us because we will live the rest of our lives alone. You brought me poetry.*
>
> *I miss you already. Good-bye.*
>
> *C*

I didn't know I would never see her again. All I knew was that the sky was cracking red in the east. Panchito hopped in and put the key in the ignition and grabbed my knee and said, "I'll run away with you, but I'm not sleeping with you." The chorus of roosters began. Fallen leaves rattled in the street, and the date palms hissed. We moved. I turned in my seat, watching the door. He said, "Let's do it in style." He turned on the tape recorder and held the mike to it. The Beatles. "Back in the USSR."

The scream of jets and Paul's scream as we sped up, scattering dogs.

And I thought I saw her, in her white gown, just that last second before we spun up the hill toward the highway, and she seemed to be in the open door, and she might have started to run after us. But we were already gone, speeding down the road that led to the graveyard, to the sea, to the north, into that terrible first light of dawn.

A DAY IN THE LIFE

FIVE A.M., and the sounds of sleeping still fill the house. Doña Juana rises first, climbing from the slumping bed as Don Manuel still snores lightly, the swollen knuckles on his left hand glistening in the dull light as blood seeps from the cracks in his leathery skin. He, like everyone else, calls her Juanita, little Juana, which has nothing to do with size and everything to do with affection. You could say it means "my little Juana."

Doña Juana sleeps in her clothes—this morning, she wears baggy Levi's provided by a gringo missionary group, new underpants worn for only two days, and a Metallica T-shirt. Although she can smell Don Manuel and the mists rising from the children and the other sleepers, she can no longer smell herself. Her breasts swing loosely under the T-shirt, long now, and nursed to the point of collapse. Her hair is turning white—lightning bolts seem to cut through her dense rope of hair, swirling down the double braid in pale corkscrews. She is missing seven teeth, and the sight of her own naked flesh alarms her. She is covered in stretch marks, scars, bites, varicose veins, and pouches of collapsed skin. She is four feet nine inches tall. She is forty-two years old.

She pulls on a battered pair of Keds dock shoes and pads out of the bedroom on her new cement floor. Manuel saved up and bought two sacks of cement. He and the neighbors made a party out of it, mixing and pouring the floor. One corner sags, but the rest of it is pretty flat. She must have one of the girls sweep: orange peels, paper, dirt, collect in the corners. She shakes her head—it's impossible to keep house. She has two rooms and a kitchen to take care of. It's too much.

She pulls aside the blanket that serves as a door as she passes into the front room. The bedroom wall wobbles as she walks through the doorway. Manuel and the boys hammered it together out of scrap wood, paper, cardboard boxes, and some water-warped *rocanrol* posters. Small pictures of Jesus, saints, and the Virgin of Guadalupe adorn the wall and cover holes. The only other decoration, in a cheap wooden frame bought in the Woolworth's downtown (they pronounce it *Goolgoort's),* is Manuel's certificate of military service. He graduated from the army a full private, and its multicolored filigree looks important to the family. It is important: an accomplishment recognized by the government. Written on the wall in Magic Marker, three inches to the right, is *"Viva Colosio, Salvador de la Gente."* This was written by Lalo, the neighbor, because neither Manuel nor Juanita knows how to write. But since Colosio was assassinated on a campaign stop downtown, he has become a beloved figure of liberation to them all. As of yet there are no plaster Colosio busts, only increasingly rare PRI-party presidential campaign posters with Russian Revolution-style portraits of the candidate staring off in the distance. The best they can do is graffiti.

They all gathered at Lalo's house to watch the assassination on Lalo's television. The gun was clear in the picture, floating out of the crowd, Lalo said, just like a bird. And they saw it: it did float out, sudden yet slow, deadly blunt, and so matter-of-fact that it looked fake. Pop. Colosio's hair mussed as if by a stiff breeze, and he fell, and their hopes toppled with him.

Lalo found his TV in the dump, and the knobs were gone, so he took knobs off another TV. The power came from a bank of salvaged car batteries and intricate wiring that only Lalo knew to connect. Manuel has been calling him the Spider because of his mad electrical webbing. But the night of the assassination, there were no jokes. Juanita wept. Nobody could understand this new thing: they have killed tomorrow in Tijuana.

"It reminds me," Manuel said, "of when the gringos killed Kennedy."

"Who?" Lalo asked.

BEHIND JUANITA, in stacked bunk beds and on a mattress on the floor, separated from Manuel by a hanging sheet, thirteen people sleep in a room twelve feet by ten feet. Of these thirteen, seven are her own children. One person, Don Manuel, is her own husband. One daughter among them, little Perla, is seven months pregnant. Two are grandchildren. One is the boyfriend of her eldest daughter, and the last two are cousins recently arrived from the garbage dump in Mexico City.

The power struggle in the Mexico City dump has driven them north, to Tijuana. The warring mafias that control the trash are locked in a subterranean *Godfather* scenario. The ancient don who ruled the trash and the trash-pickers has died, and his progeny have divided into factions, each of them battling to be King of the Trash. Gunmen and goon squads are recruiting supporters, and in its own small way, the Mexico City dump has become as complex and dangerous as the old Revolution. Trash-pickers have also had to become political analysts to survive. Like many tiny Latin American nations, the Mexico City dump has become too harsh for its citizens—they're heading north.

The young couple, sleeping together in a bottom bunk, move together under the blankets and slyly make love, rocking gently so as not to wake the others. One of the cousins, however, lies quietly in his bed and watches the woman's face as the blanket pulls away, watches her eyes roll up, close. Then a smile crosses her lips. She opens her eyes and looks right at him. He blushes, ducks his head. He hears her gasp. He thinks of home.

His name is Braulio.

THE MISSIONARIES HAVE GIVEN Doña Juana a small Coleman two-burner stove. Manuel has converted the white gas tank into a small propane system. Every week Manuel has the tank recharged downtown, at the propane tank yards. Tijuana does not have a gas system like San Diego's. Each house has a silver or white tank outside, and anyone who has grown up in Tijuana is used to the hollow ring of the tanks being loaded on and off trucks. Gas, like potable water, is delivered by ugly trucks from the 1950s and early 1960s. On delivery day, the rusty *doing* can be heard up and down the street. It's a homey sound, as sentimental as a gringo's memory of tinkling milk bottles on the porch—Mexican sounds, like the sound of the ice cream man's bell as he pushes his little two-wheeled cart along the street, the mailman's harsh whistle that sounds almost like a toy train. Doña Juana, of course, knows none of these sounds.

She turns the key and is amazed, afraid a little—as if this were some sorcery, and it probably is, because who has ever heard of such a thing. She ponders the ice that forms along the gas feed line. Wads of frost make a snowball where the line joins the burners. "Leave it to gringos," she will say, "to make ice from fire."

There is no sink. Manuel built her a counter out of a plank of plywood. Later he cut a hole in it and put a plastic tub down the hole, to hold the plates. Manuel, she thinks, is a genius. He can build anything. And the counter is covered with filthy plates, plates caked and clotted with grease and old food. Flies already work the corners of the kitchen—her one frying pan still has a fistful of fried rice and tomato in it, and has dried a sickly orange, and the flies walk over it, prod their suckers into it, and settle their rear ends deep among the hard kernels. She waves at them abstractedly, takes the pan to the front door, and dumps the rice on the dusty ground. There her piglet and a small dog fight for a bite.

No water. She hasn't bathed in a week, and there has been no water to wash things for…she can't remember. Their one water bottle, a five-gallon jug mounted on a metal frame, is half empty.

She grabs the neck of the jug, tips it, and pours cloudy water into the coffeepot.

The smell of coffee, she knows, will awaken Manuel.

And their day can begin.

FIVE-THIRTY A.M.

Don Manuel rises slowly, puts his feet on the paper-thin green carpet beside the bed, and rests his head in his hands. He has a hangover, but it's not from drinking. He doesn't know what has gotten into his head, but in the mornings there is a nauseating ache behind his forehead. It feels green to him somehow. His ears hum and his joints ache. But he won't say anything. They can't afford the doctor, and it embarrasses him to go to the missionaries. And besides, doctors are for children and women.

He sits and thinks over his list of chores for the day. Is there anything he missed yesterday? For a moment, he feels a bolt of panic—did he remember to get new rags for Juanita? It is her month again, and he promised to get her some clean cloths to make the pad. He feels a surge of adrenaline inside his body—this too is new, this sense of panic. Juanita and her blood, spilling out of her like life itself. Most couples don't talk of these things, but his old woman and he like to talk. Maybe that's what gives him the hangovers—staying up too late, whispering. There was a time, sure, when he went astray. He had sex with six women in the neighborhood, and he knows that black Cuquis bore him a son. But suddenly, and he can't explain it, Juanita became dear to him again. She was cutting the head off a chicken, and he immediately realized he loved her. She seemed so small to him then, so brave in the morning sun. The blood flew all over her arms, glistening like jewels. Though he has no word for *glisten,* he can imagine what jewels in the sun would look like.

Like sparkling red water.

His *compadre* Lalo, two shacks down, says Juanita put a love hex on Manuel. "Nobody falls back in love with their wives," he tells Manuel. "Not after all the women we have had. She gave you the *agua de coco.*"

Manuel shudders—*agua de coco* (coconut water), a brew of menses mixed in with the coffee. Which brings him back to Juana's period, and he remembers that he collected several lengths of white terrycloth at the recycling center, and she carefully folded them into pads right here on the bed. "I will be dry soon," she told him. "No more blood. No more rags. I'm an old woman."

"No more sons?" he said.

She shook her head.

Thank God, she was thinking, but she didn't tell him that.

When they had paper towels and napkins, they were the best lining to put inside the cloth pads. They could be thrown away, and the pads could last twice as long. But this month there are no napkins.

Some gringa missionaries brought down things the women stick inside themselves, but who ever heard of such a thing. They must have been Protestants. It was an insult, and probably some kind of sin. Manuel didn't know about these *cristianos* sometimes. The women had burned the terrible little objects in shame after the missionaries were gone. They wouldn't even let the children use the plastic parts for toys. Oh, well.

Manuel stretches, winces, and rises.

Braulio, the cousin from Mexico City, silently rises behind Manuel. He loves the morning, when he can think for a minute. He says his prayers, not only to Jesus and la Virgen but to the saint of his almost forgotten village in Michoacan. He can't remember the saint's name, but he can remember her face, carved in wood, her slight smile, her flaking, blue painted eyes. Braulio sits in the dull light and watches the faces of the children as they start to stir. Like the morning, the children are something he loves. He dreams of a family of his own. His fantasies include detailed plans for a new tarpaper shack. Something beautiful, something sophisticated, with a covered walkway to the outhouse and actual glass in the windows. He has figured that a central open space can be used for fires, and those fires can not only light the main room but warm the house.

He can't quite figure out how to get the smoke out without leaving an opening in the roof for rain to come in. He sees the fire in his mind. The dirt floor. The small pen in the kitchen for the ducks and chickens. It is a perfect house. When he has paper, he sketches it, placing the imaginary furniture and children in the paper rooms.

Braulio touches the face of the little girl awakening beside him. She snuffles and grimaces and slaps at his hand, rolls over. He smiles. He turns and looks across the room. He is in love with little pregnant Perla. The Pearl. The father of the baby went across the border. Perla has been waiting for him to come back, but it's obvious to everyone, even her, that he won't return. Braulio doesn't mind that she's pregnant. It's that much more work already done. She already contains his family, if she'll have him. One day he's going to have to tell her. But he gets nervous. Love does that to a man. Besides, the thought of tasting her milk arouses him, and he's sure she can sense his deviant thoughts, and it makes him feel shame. He prays to the saint to remove these desires from his heart. And he looks at Perla's smoky face and her stiff explosion of black hair on the coat she uses for a pillow, and he sighs.

Was there ever a more beautiful girl?

SIX A.M.

"Do we have anything to eat, *vieja?*" Manuel asks.

"*No, viejo.*"

She pours him a cup of black coffee. "Doughnuts?"

She pulls back her hair.

"Manuel," she says, "you know those were for the children."

"And who has to work like a mule all day?" he snaps. "The children or me?" He sips his coffee. "Besides," he says, "today is bath day. They'll get more *Doñas.*"

She sucks at her teeth for a moment, then says, "You're right."

Today the missionaries are coming. She has a crush on the pastor, *el famoso hermano,* but he doesn't even know she exists. Still, she'd like to be home, just to see him. A little flirting never hurt anybody. It doesn't mean she doesn't love her Manuelito. She looks at him, his skinny neck and his huge black mustache. He has gold trim on his teeth. My man, she thinks. But she doesn't forget her pastor, either.

She puts two stiff glazed doughnuts on the table. The missionaries collected them from a Winchell's in San Diego, and they have lain frozen in a gringo garage for a month.

"I'll get some beans too," she says. "Maybe some potatoes."

He offers her a piece of doughnut. She shakes her head.

"It's all right, *viejo*. I'm on a diet."

"Hm," he grunts. He goes to the door with his cup. "Another hot day," he says, then steps outside. He sticks his head back in the door and says, "See if the missionaries have any applesauce."

"*Ay, Dios,*" she replies. "We all know you can't live without your applesauce!"

"Every parrot to his perch," he says.

They laugh.

It makes him cough.

He turns back out the door and spits—the tiny dog at his feet barely skips away before he's hit.

SIX-FIFTEEN A.M.

He sees his *compadre,* Lalo, standing out in the street.

"*Oye, tú, pinche buey,*" he says.

"*Vete a la chingada, pinche puto cabrón,*" Lalo says. Insults taken care of, they wave and grin.

"What time are you going to work?" Manuel says.

"Now, brother."

"Well, fuck."

"No other way." Lalo shrugs.

"That's life," Manuel agrees.

"That's life."

"Life."

"Fucking life!"

"There," Manuel says, taking one last gulp of coffee, "you have said it all, *compa*. You don't have to say another word, because you have said it all right there."

He steps back inside to pull on his work shoes and collect his tools.

Manuel says to Juanita, "Lalo said *pinche* life."

"Ay, Lalo," she says.

These are Manuel's work tools: One pair of battered leather gloves, which he carries tucked into the back pocket of his pants; the way these gloves hang out and dangle is part of garbage-dump fashion. A snappy dresser will have the gloves so worn down that they're soft, and the fingers should fall flat against the man's buttocks. Although canvas gloves drape better, leather gloves are preferred.

A baseball cap to keep the sun out of his eyes.

A second pair of pants—loose and dirty dress slacks one size too big. These go on over Manuel's Levi's, as a kind of protective skin. They will catch the majority of the dump's filth and can be peeled off at the end of the day. When there's water, Juanita can boil them in a tin tub over a fire. If they get too contaminated, Manuel might drop them right there, in the trash. Often someone else will come along and pick them up: there are distinct classes among the trash-pickers, and some trash-pickers pick the castoffs of others.

Along with the second pair of pants, a shirt put on over a relatively clean T-shirt. The same rules apply: the shirt is his second skin.

A bandana for the sweat, and to be worn over the face as an occasional gas mask.

Work shoes.

Bags: bags are very valuable. Bags are Manuel's briefcase and his wheelbarrow. He will often tie a rope around his waist and tuck several plastic bags into the rope. The bags too can be a fashion statement.

The multipurpose pole carried over the shoulder like a cane fishing pole. If times are good, he might take a little lunch with him, or he might buy a festering torta or taco from a lunch wagon that brings its smoky wares into the dump. Sneaking in behind the long parade of dumptrucks, the lunch wagon pulls off to the side and opens for business. Although relatively far away from the actual garbage, the food is touched by flies and smoke and dust clouds coming out of the trash.

And these are Juanita's work tools, for she works alongside her man, everyone equal in the garbage: One clear plastic produce bag, tucked into her underwear and placed between the pads and her clothes. Otherwise, she is dressed almost exactly like her husband. Except she tucks her canvas gloves into the front of her pants. And she's worried about her shoes.

"I like these shoes, *viejo*," she says. "I hate to ruin them."

"Put bags on them," he says.

"*Estás loco.* I'll look like a fool with my feet in bags."

"That's true," he says, buttoning his pants. "You always like to look nice." He combs his hair. "I have an idea."

"What?"

"Put white bags over your shoes. That will look really good." She smiles.

"Yes," she says. "That's good. *Es muy sexy.*"

"Wow!" he says, which is his favorite word in English.

SIX-THIRTY A.M.

Braulio steps into the kitchen and says, "*Buenos días.*"

"*Buenos días,*" Manuel and Juanita say in unison.

Braulio dips his head at them, almost a bow. He still feels like an interloper, though they have made him feel at home.

"I know where I can get some eggs," he says.

"Eggs!" cries Manuel. "Who can afford eggs!"

"No money, *m'ijo,*" Juanita says.

Braulio shows them some coins that he has been storing in his pocket. They lean in and look. Manuel's eyebrows rise.

"Three gringo quarters," Braulio says, using the Spanglish word: *quattahs.* "I was going to buy a beer," he says. "But let's have eggs."

"Wow," Manuel repeats. "Wow. Yeah-yeah." He's a hipster. Braulio can't imagine being as cool as Manuel. "Shit!"

"Shat," Braulio says.

"No, shit."

"Shet."

"*No seas pendejo, socio. Shit.*"

"Chit!"

Braulio rushes out to buy a few eggs from one of the neighbors.

"He's a good boy," Juanita says.

"He's bit of a *pendejo,*" says Manuel, putting on his cap. "But he's all right."

Juanita sticks her head into the bedroom and shrieks, "Get up!"

SIX FORTY-FIVE A.M.

One of the little sisters sits on the floor in a stupor. She can never quite wake up with everyone else. She is still possessed by her dreams, and is sometimes so lost in the fog that she urinates in her pants before she manages to get up and go to the hole. She often smells of pee. Manuel calls her *huevona,* which loosely translated means "girl with big balls," which somehow means "lazy." Braulio picks her up and says, "Let's have *huevos, huevona,*" which makes her giggle. *Huevos* being eggs as well as balls. So maybe Manuel is saying she's a brood hen, sitting on eggs instead of working.

The lovers have already risen from their bunk bed and made their way out the door. They won't be seen again till evening. Off sniffing glue and smoking *mota* with the other pot-heads. Braulio doesn't know where they get money for the marijuana, though rumor has it that she lets the junkies touch her breasts for trade. Juanita and Manuel have spoken often of throwing the couple out, but they don't want to betray family.

Braulio and Perla are left in charge of the children. Everyone else, aside from the pot-heads, is outside, getting ready for work.

SEVEN-FIFTEEN A.M.

Lalo is parked outside in his pickup, angry again. He's mad every morning. "Hurry up, *cabrones!*" he shouts. Every day he wants to leave for work by seven, and every day everybody meanders around and makes him late. He would go without them, but they each pay him a few cents for rides to and from work. "The worst part about us Mexicans," he turns and tells Manuel—who is always on time—"is that we're always late."

"With any luck," Manuel replies, "we'll be late for our graves."

Lalo lights a cigarette and says, "You call that luck?"

Juanita doesn't want to ride in the cab. She prefers the bed, jammed in comfortably with eight other trash-pickers, where she can feel the wind, smell the clean scent of the ocean as they drive, see the bright colors of the *segunda,* the big outdoor flea market she usually can't afford to visit. Juanita loves to see the Pacific, sparkling and so blue, just beyond the hills. And the islands out there, right off the coast, looking so close she dreams she can swim to them. Little paradises right by the *dompe.* And the white flecks of San Diego shine on good days too, like small frozen waves on the beach.

Marilu is having trouble getting on. Juanita reaches down to her and says, "We're getting old, Mari."

"Speak for yourself," Mari says. "I'm just fat!"

They all laugh.

Lalo puts it in gear and does his best to ease over the big rocks in the road.

SEVEN TWENTY-FIVE A.M.

Lalo has stopped again, cursing and shaking the wheel. He has hit a rock and thrown Hermanita Consuelo face-first against the back window. She is easily seventy years old, though some say she is eighty. She wears girlish makeup and low-cut dresses. Her necklines reveal a chest that looks like parchment stretched over chicken bones. Her shiny bodice often reveals the acornlike stubs of her bosoms. Her lips are always bright crimson, and her cheeks are powdered pale white, and her eyes always bear heavy black pencil lines around them. She has one long orange fang in the front of her mouth. All of her children are dead, and some of the men in the barrio reportedly sneak in to visit her at night, when her husband is asleep. Consuelo still loves la Marilyn Monroe.

She has a bloody nose, and the others in the back have forced Lalo to stop. Hermanita Consuelo is spread out in the bed of the pickup, holding her nose, and all the biddies back there hover over her and cluck.

"Ay," Consuelo moans. "Ay ay."

"Poor little thing," Mari says. "That mule Lalo broke her nose."

Another pick-up pulls over and the driver calls out, "Lalo! Who did you kill this time?"

Lalo waves him off.

"A man," he says, "just can't get ahead in this world."

Manuel cranes his head around and stares at the tableau behind them.

"Poor old woman," he says.

"If she doesn't like the service," Lalo grumbles, "let her buy her own truck."

Juanita jumps down.

"I'm going to take the *hermanita* back home, all right?"

Manuel gets out of the cab and looks in at Hermanita Consuelo.

There is a dark red cut across the bridge of her nose. Her eyes are loose in her head. Blood everywhere.

"Is she all right?"

Juanita shrugs.

"She will be, if God wills it. But I'm going to take her home. She can't work like this."

"All right," he says. "Maybe the missionaries can fix her." He puts his hand on Juanita's arm. "You probably should go home anyway. You know." He glances at her belly.

"Will you be all right, *viejo*?"

"Sure. I'll be able to visit all my girlfriends without you there spying on me all day," he jokes.

She cocks an eyebrow at him and pulls away.

"Work hard," she says.

"Like a burro," he replies.

He watches his woman lead the old hag down the road, and it's hard to tell what he's feeling. He's holding up the commute, but he just stands there. Lalo has given up at this point: all the best spots will already be populated by now, and either he's going to have to sneak around till he finds a gap in the work crews or he'll have to shame himself by asking somebody if he can move in beside them. Oh, well. He was planning to make an extra couple of dollars this week for beer. He watches Manuel watching his fat little Juanita. Lalo shakes his head. It's starting to seem like Manuel thinks they have all day. Like he wants to go home with his wife.

On the radio, they're playing that damned *conjunto* punk from Mexico City, Caifanes. They're singing, "I wish I were alcohol, so I could evaporate within you."

Lalo, watching Manuel in his rearview mirror, thinks about love potions and women's fierce magics. He says, "*Agua de coco.*"

EIGHT-THIRTY A.M.

Juanita comes home and finds Perla in the kitchen, talking to Cuquis. Juanita suspects Cuquis of messing around with Manuel, but she can't prove it. Cuquis has a certain glamour in the neighborhood—she's from the east coast somewhere and has a strange accent as well as black blood. The only way she could be more exotic is if she had blue eyes and red hair. She and Perla stir as Juanita enters, and Juanita says, "Don't get up."

She tips herself a glass of water.

"The *hermanita* broke her nose."

They all tsk-tsk over the old woman's misfortune.

"No work today," says Cuquis.

"Not for her."

"Not for me," Perla says.

Cuquis stretches, says, "We were talking about being with the big belly." *Panzona.*

Perla is rubbing her abdomen. She says, "Do you know the weirdest thing about being pregnant?"

Cuquis and Juanita, who know all too much about being pregnant, smile.

"No," says Juana. "What, *m'ija*?"

"The weirdest thing about being pregnant is . . . well, there's two things. No, wait—there's *three* weirdest things about being pregnant."

Cuquis snaps, "All right! So what are they!"

Perla sticks her tongue out at Cuquis.

"*Con esa lengua,*" Cuquis says, "*mi perro se lamea el culo.*" It is so obscene that all three women burst out laughing, crying "*Ay, Dios*" and "*Ay, Cuca—no te aguantas!*"

Cuquis has told them, "With that tongue, my dog licks his asshole."

Juanita turns to heat more coffee.

"Coffee, Cuca?"

"*Sí.*"

Perla still wants to talk about her pregnancy. "First," she says, "it's my belly button. It popped out, like the baby pushed it out."

Juanita says, "He did push it out, *m'ija*. I remember mine poking out. Cuca?"

Cuquis shakes her head.

"I always have a perfect body, even when I'm pregnant."

"*Uy-uy,*" says Juanita. "You think you're so hot."

"I am hot."

Perla cuts them off. "Now it sticks out like a big thumb. My nephew saw me the other day and it was sticking out of my shirt and he said, 'Look at Auntie Perla—she has a *pipi*!'"

The women chuckle. Juanita pours them each a cup of coffee.

"And?" she says.

"The second weirdest thing is when it moves."

Juanita says, "Oh, yes."

"Restless little devils," Cuca notes.

"It kicks my liver like *a fútbol!*" cries Perla.

"They do that."

"He wants room service," Cuquis says. "He's calling for a big supper, like the actors do on television."

"*Oye,* Cuca," Juanita says, "where did you ever see television?"

"All my boyfriends," Cuquis boasts, "have televisions."

"What about your husband?"

"That good-for-nothing? No television. Why do you think I have boyfriends!"

"*Ay, Cuca!*"

"*Cuca, Cuca, eres tremenda!*"

Perla says, "And the third thing …" Worried, she looks into her own shirt. "It's my . . . *nipples.* They got so big!"

Juanita and Cuca are smiling.

"Is it normal?" Perla asks in a small voice.

"*Ay, muchacha,*" Cuquis says. "Wait until the milk comes."

"It's all right, Perla," Juanita says. "They get big—"

Cuquis: "Brown like chocolate."

"Mine are already brown, Cuca!" Perla cries.

"Then they'll get as black as old *atole.* They'll look like licorice."

Perla makes a face.

"Really?"

"These things happen, *m'ija,*" Juanita says. "God has His little surprises for women."

"I wish He'd asked me what I thought about it," Perla says.

"Don't blaspheme," Cuquis replies.

TEN A.M.

The dump itself is a vast scatter of bright specks. The trash lies across the land in layers of dull colors enlivened by exclamation points of white plastic and paper. From a hillside, it looks like a

Pollock canvas in full frenzy. And above, in swirling disks, rise the thousands of gulls. They look as if the white flecks on the ground have become animated and have begun to spiral out of the frame. So many gulls fill the bright sky that the ocean beyond is pale, as if seen through a thin bank of fog. And moving back and forth, slowly, hunched, looking like strange little birds picking insects out of the soil, the humans work. They stay silent because the noise drowns out their words. They blend with the garbage, become invisible for a moment against the camouflage. Then they move back into the sunlight—cranes, ibises, storks—but it takes effort to see them as people. And roving hugely among them, fat and wicked, exploding noxious black clouds of smoke and looking like dragons, dinosaurs, carnivorous giants, come the tractors. Big bulldozers with iron spikes on their treads, and earthmovers pulling their pregnant-looking sleds behind them. Even from a mile away, they can be heard growling, belching, coughing. At times, when the wind is right, their engines sound just like animals. Some meat-eater ripping at a corpse, the gear-shifting making them sound like they're growling. And every few bites, they pause to roar.

ELEVEN A.M.

The children have been playing in the dirt. Perla is napping. Juanita listlessly sweeps the rooms, thinking of home. She can remember poking ripe mangoes out of the trees with a long stick. Once, as a special treat, her grandmother had fried cow brains and eggs. Once she saw her mother and father making love. Once, there was a flood, and they saw a shack go by, complete, as if it had been built on the water, and there were people on the roof, crying out as they were swept into the night. These memories pass slowly through her mind. She never thinks about sex.

Braulio is outside, and he strains against a large broken wooden frame, one of the many bits of scrap and trash littering the yard, and he is thinking about sex. He overheard the women talking about breasts, and it has made him feel frantic. Perla is on his mind. He would like to sneak in the room and lie beside her. He wants to feel the roundness of her belly. He turns his back on the kids shrieking in the dirt and heaves once more against the wood. He has been wondering if he should go to school. He will have to earn money to care for Perla and his—the—baby. He isn't going to stay in the trash. He has that new house to build. He wants to buy a television. And a book. He wants to read. He wipes his brow. He wishes he had a tape recorder or a radio. Music is like reading a book with your ears. He heard a word he liked, and he feels it is true about him. Lalo said it about him, and he thinks it is the highest compliment he has ever received. The word is *filosófico*.

NOON

Huevona sits on the summit of the hill that separates the neighborhood from the rest of the world. She still smells like pee. She wears her crusty underpants, a green pair of pants under a one-piece dress, a sleeveless undershirt under the dress. Her socks are unmatched, and she wears shoes that were once white. She's watching for the missionary vans. Her smell comforts her, though she is just vaguely aware that it bothers others. They complain about it all the time. She doesn't understand why.

Clouds of dust appear below, moving steadily up the road. "*Los Americanos!*" she yells, jumping to her feet and running through the neighborhood. "*Los Americanos!*" People come out and start to hustle toward the community basketball court, where the vans will park in a semicircle. The women are already carrying their mesh and plastic bags. There are only ten men in the throng, and they are all old, sick, or drunk. All the other men are either in the trash or in San Diego.

Juanita and Perla hurry along, trying to beat the sharks. These sharks are outsiders, women who come from miles away, walking hours to get some of the American goods. There are often fistfights between locals and sharks, the women rolling around on the ground in deadly clutches, choking and punching as they roll, while their friends and neighbors laugh and taunt them and occasionally kick them.

The bathing rooms are already waiting. The gringos pay a small rent to two families for the use of their buildings. One of them, Hermana Josefina, is a Mixtec Indian who has managed to eke out a good living from the generosity of the gringos. When they are visiting, she is the humblest and saddest Christian woman, cooing things like "I am God's poorest little child" to the translators. When they're gone, she likes her *mezcal* and her cigars, becomes a tyrant, and uses her imagined position of power to coerce and threaten the neighbors into doing her bidding.

Her latest ploy is to convert her small barn into a church, which various evangelical groups use for services and Bible studies. Each group pays Josefina, if not in money, in clothes and food and soda cans and prestige. The current gossip about her is that she is a Satanist and that she works black magic on her enemies. Cuquis whispers to Juanita that Josefina has sacrificed a baby. Someone or other saw it, it's true.

"I heard," Juanita says, "that she has sex with the Devil." Cuquis and Perla look at each other and nod: there is no doubt about it. Perla makes the sign of the cross, lest Josefina give her the evil eye—*el mal de ojo*—and somehow harm the baby within her. Babies have been born with horns, tails. Everyone knows it's true. She shudders, even though the sun has already burned the hilltop into the high eighties.

"Old witch," she mutters.

Josefina has a different take on the situation. She can remember when she gave birth in that same little barn they use for church. She was alone, no one there even to hold her hand. And she remembers cutting the umbilical cord herself, with a kitchen knife. And she remembers almost losing that same baby to a terrible pox that the missionaries cured with an injection and cans of fluid that she threw away because the color looked evil to her.

She remembers her mother being kicked in the stomach by

Mexicans just like these women. Why shouldn't she have something extra? Nobody but her takes in abandoned Indian children. She even feeds orphaned *mestizo* kids, though she doesn't love anyone outside her tribe. Except the missionaries. She loves them quite a bit. Her favorites are the Baptists, though she is Catholic. The Baptists have the best doughnuts.

Josefina has her own family to feed plus three new orphan boys. Let them talk all they want. None of them had the strength of will to force their husbands to build a barn. You keep a man too busy to do mischief, and you have to be stronger than him. Take control and keep them scrambling—anybody knew that much.

And as long as the gringos don't know that she has the biggest pigpens in the area—hidden down the back side of the hill—they will take pity on her. For the situation in Mexico has reduced urban Mixteca women to one thing: begging. They stand in traffic in every big Mexican city, and if they are lucky, they have a baby at their breast. Their greatest art, now that their pyramids are gone and forgotten and their cities laid to waste and overgrown with weeds and jungles, is pity. Everything depends on how abject they can look, how piping and pitiable their voices, how huge their eyes. How much of their breast is revealed as the baby suckles. The tribal women, called Marias by the Mexicans, have learned to massage the appalling sentimentality of gringos and *mestizos*. While the modern world grinds them like corn, its operators occasionally feel saddened by the big black eyes and toss out a few cents. Josefina is only doing what Mexico has told her she must do. She begs. But she will not grovel. Let the missionaries fill her gut and cover her back. Let the women of the barrio fear her.

She says to her friends, Why shouldn't I have power over these damned Mexicans?

When no one is listening, she sings songs in her own tongue.

ONE P.M.

Boys shuffle off to Josefina's barn. There, men have set up curtained shower stalls made from galvanized tubs and PVC piping.

The girls wander down the road to a small house with a real floor. Astonishingly robust Baptist women stomp around making loud noises and wide gestures. The Mexican and Indian women surreptitiously gawk at these golden beings, wondering how they get so shiny, how they manage to stay clean and get so tall. Their eyes are often blue, their skin peachy and smooth. You can smell them from a meter away: perfume, deodorant, mint chewing gum, shampoos and conditioners and whatever other lotions they have smeared on themselves. None of them smell like pee, sweat, or bad teeth. Their breasts are pointy and as hard as fruit, it's obvious. They have big solid asses, and they all seem to love Jesus, even when they don't always give evidence of loving the poor. The neighbors think the gringo men are often cute, if a little soft. But these gringas. It's like a television set has broken open and these bellowing female giants have stormed out among real people. Every woman in line is happy that their men are away, at work. And Juanita is keeping her eye open for her favorite, the pastor.

Fifty-one other women watch for him too.

ONE-THIRTY P.M.

The children are shampooed first. They line up and dip their heads into tubs as more *americanos* splash water and shampoo on them. Many of the kids have lice, so there is a lot of Kwell lice-killing shampoo in the water. Many mothers don't want their children to be washed here, because it doesn't take long for the tub to look like it's full of Nestle's Quik, chocolate and thick and floating with dying lice. Babies scream and kick. And the young Bible student volunteers laugh and sparkle and curse in the weirdly gutted fashion of evangelicals: Gosh! Dang! Gosh darn it! Darn you! Oh good gosh!

After the shampoo, it's off to the baths. And after the baths, the children receive their treats. Each gets a bag with two doughnuts, two or three pieces of fruit, and a carton of cold chocolate milk the color of their bathwater. They have each earned a few points, paid in poker chips and rubber stamps on the backs of their hands. With these points, they can purchase candy, or popcorn, or even small toys and toothbrushes, at the *bodega* set up in one of the vans.

For most of the mothers, these afternoons are the only times they have freedom. Their men are gone, and someone else is caring for their children. They gather and gossip, flirt, show off, fight. They line up at various vans to receive their goods. After they have gone through the line, they run to the end and hope there is enough left for seconds. Sly women send their children into other lines, and they switch places, sometimes sending family members through three or four times. These are the venture capitalists of the neighborhood.

Hermana Josefina outrages them all by refusing to enter any line. She stands near the door of her barn and smiles at them like some benign queen vaguely amused by their antics. She makes a great show of hugging the pastor as he tries to enter the barn. Her skin is almost black against his grizzled white arms. Her eyes, peeking around him and flashing at the women in the lines, are as impenetrable as obsidian.

Cuquis nudges Juanita.

"That old witch is stealing your man."

The other women laugh.

Juana ignores them and turns to Perla.

"Little Mother," she says. "What about Braulio?"

"What about him?"

"Well? What about him?"

"Braulio?"

"Yes."

"Our Braulio?"

"He's the only Braulio I know."

"Oh," Perla says, looking off. "He's not horrible."

"Do you like him?"

"I don't like being alone."

"But do you like *him*?"

"Maybe."

"Think about him," Juanita says. "I like him for you."

"Braulio," Perla repeats.

Cuquis looks at her and grins.

"What's your problem?" Perla snaps.

CUQUIS CAN READ. She pores over a Bible the missionaries have given her.

"Listen to this," she says. " 'Let the rich man glory in his humiliation, because like flowering grass he will pass away. For the sun rises with a scorching wind and withers the grass. And its flower falls off. And the beauty of its appearance is destroyed. So too the rich man in his pursuits will fade away.' "

Several of the women mutter, "Amen."

"Good old Jesus Christ," Cuca says. "He'll kick the shit out of those rich bastards."

ONE FORTY-FIVE P.M.

The van doors swing open. The women surge, almost break out of line and rush ahead in a little riot, but they already know that at the first sign of pandemonium, the doors will close and the food will drive away. Two weeks without provisions. So they shove each other and jostle a bit and hiss and tsk and mutter, but they hold formation.

They each receive:

—*One kilo of pinto beans, weighed and poured into a brown paper lunch bag*

—*Six potatoes*

—*Three onions*

—*One kilo of long-grain rice, also poured into a brown paper bag*

—*A few apples or oranges or bananas.*

They are in luck today! The next van has canned food. It's a strange mixture, and some of it will have to go to the pigs because nobody knows what to do with it.

Veg-All. Creamed corn. Pear halves. Pumpkin pie filling. Pickled beets. Spam. Corned beef hash. Beefaroni. Tuna. Sauerkraut. Carnation condensed milk. Smoked oysters. Something without a label, flecked with rust. Alpo.

"What's this?" says Perla, holding up a small can. It says *Escargots.*

"Look at the picture," says Juanita.

Perla makes a face.

"The picture has snails on it."

Juanita grabs the can and stares at it.

"My God," she says. "Gringos eat bugs."

"I'm going to barf," Perla says.

They throw the can away.

THREE-THIRTY P.M.

The pastor has felt guilty for years, watching the women stand in these ragged lines, waiting. He wants to make them happy, not just to feed them or preach to them. It has recently occurred to him to give them a carnival. He has invested some money and a lot of time in creating a series of midway games for the mothers to enjoy—*competencias,* they call them. There is a balance beam and a beanbag toss, pitching games and even a game with ray guns and bleeping flashing targets. The women compete for candy bars and Cokes. They have grown to love the games, and they hurry from the food lines to line up and take aim with their three beanbags.

Juanita waits for the pastor to come out of the bathing room. When he finally does step out, in a hurry as always, she feels a thrill. He is the tallest man she has ever hugged, and she throws her arms around him before he can get away. He can't speak a lick of Spanish, and he does his best, patting her on the back and saying, "*Ah! Sí, sí! Hola! Muy bien!*" as he tries to escape her grip. He has two more orphanages to get to today, and they're running a half-hour late as it is.

"Hermano," she says as he pulls away. "Hermana Consuelo is hurt."

The pastor waits for the translator to repeat it, then he asks, "How hurt?"

"*Cabeza,*" says Juanita, indicating the head. "*Mucha sangre.*"

The pastor understands this perfectly well. He has seen a swimming pool's worth of *sangre* these last thirty years.

"*Muy mal,*" Juanita says. "*Está en su cama.*"

"She's in bed," the translator says, sounding like a monkey to Juanita. "Real bad."

The pastor looks at his watch, sighs, says, "Let's go take a look."

Juanita is thrilled when he puts an arm lightly on her shoulders as they pass the lines of neighbors and sharks. She looks back at Cuquis and Perla and scrunches her nose at them, wiggles her hips. The pastor is oblivious: he's wondering when the hell he'll get a chance to eat something.

In the doorway behind them, Josefina is fuming.

FOUR P.M.

They collect Braulio as they walk. The pastor likes Braulio—he can see a good heart in him. "Broolio," he says, the translator behind him like an echo, "you're a winner. You're a special boy." Braulio blushes. It's like God sticking a gold star on your homework.

Homework.

"Pastor," he blurts, "I want to go back to school!"

The pastor smiles.

"Well, let me see what I can do about that."

Braulio can't believe his ears.

"*Gracias,*" he says.

"*Ah! Sí! Bueno, bueno!*" the pastor enthuses.

They knock at Hermana Consuelo's doorway. They can hear her old husband, Pepe, blind and *muy loco,* shuffling around inside.

"*Mamá, Mamá,*" he is saying. "'*onde 'sta Mamá?*"

They step in, and Braulio's mouth drops open. He moves behind the pastor and hides. Juanita touches the pastor's arm and then crosses herself. It takes them a second to figure out what they see, but in the cramped gloom of the shack, the terrible scene reveals itself: blind Pepe, immensely fat and shirtless, is tied by the wrist to the center pole that holds up the roof. The rope has cut into his skin, and he has walked around and around the pole, like a tied dog, until he has come up tight against the pole and can't move.

"Where's Mama?" he asks. "Where's Mama?"

Hermana Consuelo is lying on her back on their nearly black mattress, dead. Her mouth is open, full of congealed blood. Blood has run from her nostrils, forming a black mustache. Her eyes stare. Flies hurry along her lips, pausing occasionally to scrub their hands. Braulio doesn't want to cry, but he bursts into tears anyway, and Juanita takes him against her breast, where he sobs.

The pastor covers Consuelo's face with her blanket and takes out his knife and cuts Don Pepe loose.

He lightly embraces Juanita and Braulio and says, "Let's step outside now and leave her alone."

The translator forgets to say anything.

FIVE P.M.

The gringos are gone.

The pastor has given Braulio a ride over to the dump to collect Don Manuel. Nobody knows what to do, but Manuel and Lalo will think of something. The pastor has left $100 with Josefina to help pay for the burial. "Fina!" Juanita snaps. "She'll steal the money!"

As the gringos drive away, and as Perla, against all orders, steps inside to look at Consuelo's body and Juanita and Cuquis lead poor crazy Don Pepe to Juanita's house, one of Fina's nieces breaks away from the crowd to tell her what Juanita has been saying about her.

Braulio wades through the trash, looking for Manuel. He finally spots him by a stack of bulging bags. Manuel has pulled off his gloves, and he's drinking water from a plastic jug, waiting for Lalo to come collect him and take him home.

"Uncle!" Braulio calls.

Manuel looks over at him and waves for him to come closer.

"What brings you to the *dompe?*" Manuel asks.

"Doña Consuelo!" Braulio cries. "She died!"

"What do you mean, she died?"

"She's dead. All full of blood. Her mouth and nose."

Manuel whistles.

Braulio says, "She drowned in her own blood, it looks like! I thought I was going to be sick!"

Manuel hands him the water jug, and Braulio takes a drink. Manuel puts his hand on Braulio's shoulder and says, "Now listen. When Lalo comes, you don't say anything. I'll tell him. You keep quiet. All right?"

Braulio nods.

"Not a word," Manuel says.

"No."

They wait.

Soon Lalo comes banging along the dirt track that runs along-side the dump. He waves out the window at them. He parks and gets out.

"Another no-good long goddamned day," he says, smiling his wild pirate's smile.

"Lalo," Manuel says. "Come here for a minute."

He leads Lalo off to the side, puts his arm around his shoulders, and puts his face near his *compadre's*. Lalo pulls away. "What!" Braulio hears him shout. Then Manuel speaks to him some more. Lalo puts his hand over his eyes. He lowers himself to the ground and sits with his head hanging and his eyes covered. When Manuel says something else to him, he swings his arm blindly, throwing a wild punch that rakes in only air. Silently, Manuel sits beside his friend and looks at the tractors making their way out of the clouds of seagulls.

SEVEN P.M.

All Lalo could say when he got home was "I'm sorry. I'm sorry." They all told him it wasn't his fault, but he feels the guilt crushing him. And he has begun to wrestle with the debt he now owes. Must he now care for Don Pepe? Can he care for the old madman? He knows the least he can do is build Consuelo a coffin. He is afraid to see her, afraid to face what his carelessness has done, for he is a man of conscience, and he knows his impatience killed her. "Don't make me look at her," he begged Manuel. "I can't. I can't."

Later, he knows, he will be drunk. Very, very drunk. But not yet. He has work to do. Manuel has taken him off to buy wood. It's the least he can do.

Consuelo's house is dark. Lit candles sputter before her door, and several women, led by Cuquis, say a rosary outside. Their quiet voices sound like muffled music. Juanita's house is bright. Lit up, with the door open. Everyone in the barrio has been coming around to leave money with her. Most of them give Don Pepe a hug. He chuckles; he thinks it's his birthday or Christmas. "Oh!" he cries with each hug. "Hello! Hello!"

Juanita collects the sums in a coffee can, and Perla carefully scratches each person's name on a piece of notebook paper. Braulio sits across from her and watches.

"What are you looking at?" she says.

"You," he replies.

"Why?"

"You're beautiful."

She puts down her pencil and looks at him for a long while.

Juanita has tied Don Pepe to a chair. She spoon-feeds him warm creamed corn. He smacks his lips. The children are terrified of him.

Huevona peers out from behind the cloth bedroom door, wide-eyed. She smells like Ivory soap and baby shampoo. She hates smelling so sweet.

Don Pepe smells like wet cigars.

Juanita calls to her.

"You, Huevona! Come here."

She steps into the room, cutting a wide detour around smelly Don Pepe.

"Where's Mamá?" he asks the blank air.

"The pastor gave that witch Fina one hundred dollars to help pay for the funeral."

Huevona nods her head, wide-eyed. She always looks like a deer, or a wildcat.

"Go up there and collect it for me," Juanita says. "Tell her we have all the burial money here, and we are keeping a record of who pays so we can show the pastor we did our part."

Huevona nods.

"Do you understand?"

Huevona nods again.

"Then get going!" Juanita claps her hands. Huevona jumps. She takes Braulio's hand and tugs. He resists for a second.

"Don't worry," Juanita says. "La Perla will still be here when you come back."

Both Braulio and Perla blush.

When he steps out with the little girl, everyone, even crazy Don Pepe, is laughing.

Across town, Lalo and Manuel are working in Lalo's cousin's yard. They have several planks of raw pine between them, and they are cutting them up with a borrowed saw. Though they are still horrified over Consuelo's death, they are also getting the giggles. Lalo's cousin has poured two beers down their throats already, and he has gone to get some tequila.

"Goddamn it, Lalo," Manuel says. "Did you have to kill her tonight? I was going to make love to Juanita!"

Lalo falls down laughing.

"Stop it! You're killing me!"

"Look who's talking," Manuel says.

JUANITA LOOKS UP as fat Mari stops by.

"I only have fifty cents," Mari says, "but I brought something for Don Pepe."

"*Mamá?*" Don Pepe asks, his poached-looking eyes rolling back and forth.

"No, old man, it's me, Marilu." She kisses him on the head. "I brought you some candy."

"Oh!" He laughs. "Candy!"

She unwraps a Tootsie Roll Pop and puts it in his mouth. He sucks it like a baby.

"Mari," Perla says as she writes down *Marilu, cincuenta centavos*.

"Gringos eat bugs."

"You don't say."

"It's true! We saw a can of snails this afternoon."

"*Dios mío*," Mari says. "Leave it to gringos to cook snails."

All the women pause to shake their heads.

EIGHT-THIRTY P.M.

Abandoned, the coffin lies half finished. Lalo is asleep. Manuel and Lalo's cousin are drunk and singing love songs. Tears run down Manuel's cheeks. It does not occur to him to go home. He takes the bottle. The tequila rips down his throat like a bare electric wire. "I don't give a shit," he says to no one, no one at all.

NINE P.M.

Braulio and Huevona slink into the house. Juanita sees them and turns in her chair. Josefina is standing in the doorway, smoking a cigar. She blows smoke into the room. They can smell her: she's been drinking.

"Fina," Juanita says, nodding. "Come in."

Josefina stands there, unmoving. Smoke leaks out of her nostrils like something alive and greasy. It crawls up her face and over her hair. Perla coughs.

"The smoke bothers me," she says.

"Don't talk back to me, *morra*," Josefina says.

Perla, never one to pass up a fight, says, "How can I talk back when you haven't said anything?"

Josefina takes one step forward.

"Do you need to learn some manners?" she asks.

Braulio rises and extends his hands, making peace.

"*No hay pedo,*" he says, the absurd lower-class slang for "There's no trouble here," which can only be translated as "There is no fart between us."

"*Calma.*"

Juanita watches, tense, ready to jump.

Don Pepe is asleep, his sad rocky head hanging, drool falling onto his chest.

"Fina," Juanita says. "Did you bring the money?"

"Money," Fina says, and turns her deadly red eyes toward Juana. "Money. I hear you think I'm a thief."

Juana casts her eyes down.

"I hear," Fina says, rolling the cigar in her mouth, smelling of ferment and fire, "you think I'm a witch."

Braulio steps toward her and makes the mistake of touching her arm.

"Fina—" he manages to say before she shocks him with a right-handed roundhouse slap that knocks him off his feet.

Inside Juanita's house, it looks like there has been an explosion.

Braulio falls.

Huevona screams and runs.

The other children scream and scatter.

The little dog bursts out from under the table, barking.

The table tips over.

Piglets fly like shrapnel.

Juanita flies out of her seat and strikes Fina.

Perla, shrieking like a cat, throws herself over Braulio, who is crawling across the floor, and tackles both women.

They hit the floor in an avalanche of chairs and plates and forks and billowing skirts.

Pepe wakes up with a start and cries out, "Mama! Where is Mama!"

Screams, grunts, smacks, curses, crashes, shatterings, thuds, snarls.

Pepe tries to get up, still tied to the chair, yelling for Mamá to come get him, and the women roll into him and knock him over backward.

Braulio staggers to his feet, turns the wrong way, and plunges through one of the paper walls.

Manuel's framed military diploma falls and the glass breaks.

Juanita has Fina by the hair, and she is punching her in the face. Punching, punching, hammering.

Fina throws a kick that catches Perla in her huge pregnant stomach, and Perla staggers back, clutching herself, almost retching, and she hits the Coleman stove, and the boiling pot of rice flies to the floor, scalding everyone, and the gas-feed line breaks, and a terrible hissing escapes, and flames billow high, scrabbling up the wall.

They all pause for the slightest moment, listening to this strange sound, before they try to run out the door.

Yelling for the children.

Perla screaming, "Braulio!"

And Braulio steps back into the room as the gas bottle explodes and blows him backward, right out through the wall of the bedroom.

NINE-THIRTY P.M.

Everyone stands and watches Juana's house burn. One of the piglets is trapped inside and is screeching as it burns. Perla holds her hands over her ears. Braulio tries to hug her and all the children at once. Everyone is weeping. Fina, blood on her face, sheepishly comforts Juanita.

"I'm sorry," she says, made sober by the fire. "Want a cigar?"

Juana counts heads—everyone is accounted for except for Manuel and the pot-head couple. Well, they're all off drunk somewhere, and thank God for that.

The firemen don't get there until ten-thirty. Someone has had to run a half-mile to the phone booth beside the general store. The firemen are contacted, but it takes quite a while to explain where the fire is. The firemen have had to traverse downtown Tijuana, then rush south on a two-lane road.

They've been driving around the hills, trying to discover the dirt road up here, and by the time they arrive, the fire has almost burned itself out. It gutters and smolders, but it's down to the ground. They hardly have to spray any water on it at all.

"Perla," Juana says. "Did you save the money?" Perla holds up the coffee can.

"*Gracias a Dios*," Juana says.

Don Pepe sits in the dirt, sucking his Tootsie Roll Pop. Everything is gone.

MIDNIGHT

The neighbors return now, each carrying a small item to give to Juanita: an undershirt for Manuel when he gets home, a bag of powdered doughnuts, a blanket, a pillow, three eggs, a battered old pot, a cigarette, a bottle of rum, a coat, a potato, wet panties just washed and wrung out.

"They're almost new," the woman says to Juana. "They have flowers on them."

Juana hugs her. Juana hugs many people. Some of them have only hugs to offer.

Cuquis and the funeral prayer circle have moved nearer to Juana's clan, and they now pray for them.

Juanita is too tired to cry.

Braulio and Fina have gone to Fina's barn and collected a heavy sheet of plastic. Braulio has an idea. Fina's sons help him haul the sheet back to Juana's yard. Everything stinks of smoke. Everything and everybody is black.

"Glory to God," Juana repeats often. "We are all safe. Everybody's all right."

"At least we're together, Mamá," Perla says.

"Glory to God. Glory to God."

Braulio has seen that the wooden frame he moved away from the house is safe, unburned in the far corner. He drags it forward, around the glowing embers of the house, and he says, "I can build us a tent."

Amazed, Juanita and Perla watch Braulio take charge of all the men who stand around gawking.

"All right, you lazy bastards," he says, sounding exactly like Manuel, "we have work to do."

And they get to work.

TWO A.M.

The children are asleep in an unruly pile on the clothes that the neighbors have brought. Cuquis has taken poor old Don Pepe home with her. He will escape while she sleeps, however, and will be discovered without his pants in the morning, wandering around the basketball court. The moon can be seen through the clear plastic lean-to Braulio has constructed. He looks over at Juanita: she sleeps in the dirt, her head on the one pillow. In her hand is the charred corner of Manuel's diploma.

Carefully, trying to make no sound, he scoots over closer to Perla. She sleeps on her side, with her knees drawn up, and one hand covers her mouth. He stares at her in the gloom. He cries, looking at her. He longs to put his mouth on her mouth and to feel her hot breath inside his mouth. He imagines it tastes sweet. He wants to take her heavy hair in his hands and squeeze it.

He thinks, as he often thinks, if she will just marry him, he will show her what kind of a man he is. Or can be, anyway. He is only fourteen. Perla is thirteen.

Braulio's transistor radio is murmuring softly beside them. That *conjunto pop* from Mexico City, Mana, is singing. They say, "You are my religion."

He'll build her the dream house. He'll work every day.

He'll get her a television.

And a pig.

He'll make new babies inside her.

He'll plant flowers in their yard.

He'll die for her.

He moves close to her, carefully, carefully—his jaws ache with the tension. And he maneuvers himself under her tattered blanket, wanting to feel her heat as she sleeps. Wanting to be near her. He can't stop crying. He stretches himself out on the ground beside her and closes his eyes. He can smell her sweat. He leans close and lightly lets his lips touch her hair.

He is startled when her hand reaches out and clasps his. Silently she pulls his fingers toward her belly, moves them up and down on the taut softness of it. Then she moves his hand up to her breast and cups herself with his hand and snuggles in against him and goes back to sleep.

Braulio lies awake, stiff, afraid to move, afraid to breathe.

All he can think to do is pray.

FIVE A.M., and snuffling and snoring fills the tent.

Doña Juana wakes first, and for a brief moment she can't remember what happened. She sits up and is startled to see the ruins, the tent, the children tucked in around her. She is also startled to see Perla caught up in Braulio's arms and their legs tangled together. She looks up and sees a burly shadow through the plastic. She crawls out and looks into Manuel's eyes.

"Are you all right?" he asks.

"We're all safe," she says.

Manuel hangs his head.

She goes to him.

"There is nothing you could have done, *viejo.*"

"I'm sorry, is all," he replies, taking her in his arms. "I'm sorry."

Lalo is keeping his distance.

He is ready to help, but he is not sure what is to be done. "I saved this for you," Juana says, handing Manuel the corner of the diploma. "Everything else is gone."

"Everything?"

"Everything."

Manuel turns to Lalo and says, "Everything is gone."

"Everything?"

"Everything."

"*Chingue a su madre,*" Lalo says.

Juana says, "Braulio has some good ideas."

"Braulio!"

"He was the hero. He took charge. And he has ideas for a new house."

"Braulio," Manuel says. "Imagine that."

"He's a philosopher," Lalo calls. "Smart."

Juana says, "He's going to be your son-in-law, I think."

Manuel throws his hands in the air.

"Did anything not happen while I was gone?" he cries.

"Jesus Christ didn't return, looks like," Lalo says.

Manuel glares at him.

"Come," Juanita says to her man. "Rest with me."

"I can't rest!" Manuel says. "Look at this! Our lives are gone."

"*No, viejo,* our lives are here." She puts her hand on his chest. "Our lives are here, no? Our things are gone, that's all."

"Yeah," says Lalo. "You didn't have anything anyway. Screw it."

Manuel just looks at him.

Lalo shrugs.

"You know. Another *pinche* day of life, *compadre,*" he offers.

Then he walks to his own house.

Manuel nudges Juana. She looks up at him.

"I brought you a flower," he says.

He pulls a battered rose out of his pocket.

"Oh, you," she says, taking it and holding it to her chest. "My little old man."

They hold each other and weep softly, looking over the smoking gray and black charcoal pit that was their house. Juana pulls him tight and rocks him back and forth. She speaks into his chest, so he doesn't hear her at first. She has to repeat herself.

She says, "Next time we build a house, let's plant a garden. Let's plant roses." She's thinking of Braulio, of his dreams and his ideas. She smiles into Manuel's ribs.

"Roses," she says. "They're like music for your eyes."

And Manuel closes his eyes for a moment and listens: small birds are singing all over the hill. Where do they hide, all the little birds? Why don't they fly across the border, where the gringos probably throw food all over the streets? So many songs in the cool air—so many tiny, insistent, hopeful voices.

"These birds, I think," he says, "all speak Spanish."

"What are they saying?" she murmurs.

"They're saying, 'Hey—at least it's not raining.'"

FATHER RETURNS
FROM THE MOUNTAIN

THE CAR IS RED. It has a sun-baked and peeling black top. Little flakes of fake leather blow away in the wind. The roof is crushed. Windows are shattered. The front end is crumpled. The axles are split and the tires slant crookedly. Dry blood on the hood. The steering wheel is twisted. Details of violence. An American Motors Rambler 440, 1966 model. Slivers of glass are stuck in the carpets. Dust settles on the stains. A photograph of my father and me is caught under the seat, fluttering like a flag, like a bird trapped in the wind. There is a dime in the broken driver's seat. Blood where the radio should be. / This is the truth. The truth is a diamond, or at least a broken mirror. There are many reflective surfaces, and we observe the ones we choose. We see what we can. / The car is red. It stands in a dusty compound among other crushed machines. A note to my father in a flowery woman's hand blows out of the glove compartment. It whispers "Querido Alberto" a hundred times as it spins away. There is a chain-link fence that rattles in a breeze that smells of dogs and perfume. A yellow sticker is pasted to the hood because there is no glass to hold it. Children scare each other by touching the crusty patches of my father's blood. "He'll come back to eat you!" The dead man, the dead man. / A Mexican cop slides down the slope. He squints in the early morning sun. He can hardly see my father in the wreckage. He runs back up and calls for help. The blue light atop his car flashes, flashes, casting marching shadows over the rocks. Pink urine spreads across my father's clothing. The pain is a sound that hums inside his gut, that pierces his skull. Darkness. Sleep. / The telephone feels warm. I look out the window at a Monday sky. "Hello," he says. It is a family friend. "Do you remember me?" The morning sunlight reaches through the trees. "Of course I remember you. What's up?" His silence buzzes for a moment. When he speaks, he speaks carefully. "Your father…has had an accident." "Is he hurt?" "Yes." "Badly?" "Yes." I lean forward. I think of my father being hurt. I think of him in pain. The tiny agony of tears pinches the corners of my eyes. / We are on a balcony in Puerto Vallarta. I am in love with the most inconceivable girl in Rosario, Sinaloa. Ebony crabs have come in from the jungle, mad with the rain that hasn't stopped for two days. They climb the stairs of the hotel, wait before our doors, attack us when we come out. His hand is on my shoulder. I cannot contain the feelings as we watch lightning bombard the hilltops. Rain undermines the streets and floods the river that eats great rifts in the jungle. We spend the entire night in each other's confidence. And when the tears come, he lets me cry. / My father is severely damaged. His eyes are open, but will not function. They scrape up and down, but they cannot break the thick shell of darkness that covers them. His body will not move—he tells it to—to get the hell up, get back in the car, light a cigarette, go bowling, something. Anything. But he is frozen. His mouth is a traitor that will not function. It fills slowly with liquid. When it reaches his lips, there is a gradual, endless snail of red slipping down his cheek and hiding in his ear. I am sitting in my room listening to music. / "How bad?" I ask, a little afraid, a little unwilling, a little uncertain. "Very bad. He flew off a mountain. He fell in the desert." The sun is bright. / The car is red. The police compound is quiet. A scrawny cat licks the speedometer. / The police lift him into the ambulance. He tries to talk, he tries to see he is a slab of meat and it makes him angry. The pain makes him angry. The cuts on his face sting. And through the morning, dawn scorching the paper-sheet horizon, ravens smelling the blood and exploding off the road before them, the ambulance crew flies. To a hospital—well, a clinic. Scorpions drowsing in its shade. And there, the nurses find him almost dead, and strip him bare, and shoot a load of morphine in his fallen veins, and tie him down in case he kicks, and leave him naked eight hours alone. He knows he's naked—God, he's mad. But the poppies blooming in his arms send out their odors, their perfume already bubbles up his throat, and down, down, beyond his belly, to where the memories dwell. The blood has made his throat black. / I sit alone in the funeral home. There is little sound from without: even downtown Tijuana has to sleep. 3:00 a.m. No sleep for me. Me and the body, we're wired. / I open the coffin lid and look at him. He is broken. His chin is a black openness. He was always shaved pink and now little gray whiskers are pushing their heads up through the wounds. His shirt is stained. I put my face to the side of the box and stare and stare. I watch for a flicker, a twitch. I wait for a microscopic flare of the nostrils. The sealed eyelids seem ready to pop, to rise and lower. I want, in terror, to see him lick his lips so that I can break the Mexican sealing glass, pull him up, save him, embrace him. There is no movement. There is no sound. / I found a photograph just yesterday. In it, my father stands with the president, with generals, senators. His captain's uniform looks as crisp as a salad. At times, I shuffle through his official papers and look at his federal police badge. His smiles look like mine. We are connected by the lips. The grin is our chain. / I lie on the floor beneath the coffin. He's up on a table laid out like God's buffet. I close my eyes to sleep, my last night beside him. I am a poet at that instant. A shadow passes over my face. I jump up, thinking that someone is approaching. There is nothing. Again the shadow. Again nothing. Again and again. I imagine him waving farewell. As I slip into sleep, I have a vision of a stiff hand reaching for me over the edge. / The dreams have come in a series. They are diamonds. They are broken mirrors. In the first, I am run over by a truck. My half-brother stands on the curb and smiles down at me. I pull at people's legs from the black street. / Death is here now. I am finally aware of it. Perhaps childhood is not knowing that it is grinning at you from the corner. It has pressed its face against the windows, it has stalked in with the fog and awaits its turn. / At 8:00 p.m. he tried to open his eyes. His straining led to nothing. My father was born in Rosario, little gem at the southern end of Sinaloa. He died in San Luis Rio Colorado, a dry husk in the north of Sonora. I can imagine his gray hair against the pillow. His lips, white, rolling back almost in a smile. His abdomen searing red hot, then tingling pink as he passed through to the new side. Possibly music, a fragment of a tune wafting through the haze. I hope he heard music. / The family friend calls again. "Tell me," I say. "His condition deteriorated for several hours." "And?" "And your señor…rested." "Dead?" "Dead." "Just now?" "Yes." "Thank you." "Are you all right?" "Thank you." / No one comes to the funeral home to spell me. It's a wake, and I'm awake. I have watched the corpse for seven hours. I have closed the lid. I have not eaten since the day before. "I hate waiting," I say out loud. His voice: "I know, Son. I always hated it too. It's boring." I spin around, but the lid remains closed. There's nobody else in the room. "Do you hear me?" I ask. "Yes," he replies. "I love you," I say. "I know," he says. / Mexicans love the dead. They are a lovely treat with which to terrify each other. Dawn's light, and people passing in the street push open the door to peek at the coffin. "What are you looking at, you vampires?" I yell at them. "El muerto," they whisper. "El muerto." / We carry the coffin to the graveside. I have to go to the bathroom. Dogs are running on the graves. Whores and cops and ice cream men are working downtown. People are eating and laughing and sweating and making love all over the world and my father is dead. The world has not even hesitated. Nobody has noticed. / The hard part is watching the box go down. Watching it being pushed into the black mouth, knowing that his flesh is being hid from you, and if you should search for a touch of it again you will find dusty corruption. The body goes. I walk away from the weeping. White clouds on the border. I keep my back to the mourners. Tijuana looks pretty from a distance. I was born there. / I sit in my house alone, working on the third draft of a book no-one will ever read. I hear a car in the driveway. When I open the door, the car is red. My dead father is leaning on the steering wheel. His hair is in disorder, his eyes are uncertain. I go to him, take his cold hand, lead him inside. He sits on the couch, settling like a white feather. "What happened?" he asks. I look into his face. He doesn't know. He doesn't know he's dead. Maybe I can fool him. Keep him alive. But I know as I hope it is impossible. I kneel at his feet. "Papá, you were killed." "Killed! But I'm right here!" "You were killed in an accident." "But the car's in the driveway. Brand new." "No." "It can't be," he says. I am afraid of hurting him, but I must. "Papá," I say, "go away. You're dead." "I can't be dead," he insists, pain and frustration mixing on his face. / As a child, I would ride standing beside him as he drove, holding tight to his shoulder. / I take his pant-legs in my hands. "Papá, go away. You can't stay here. You're dead!" He shakes his head sadly. I weep like his little boy wept, with my head on his knees. "You're dead, you're dead, you're dead." / A stonemason gets in the grave and spreads concrete over the box. We don't have enough money for a headstone. Maybe a tree will grow here, or a stand of mustard, goldenrod. Other mourners file in to feed the hole beside my father's. / The car is red. The cold desert wind moans in it at night. There is a scar on the mountain where he crashed. His glasses bend the moonlight between the crumbled rocks. / I hear his engine again. He looks much better. "Get in," he says. I get in. He takes me through miles and miles of dreamlands. Things that do and do not exist pass by, one after one. We are free to go anywhere we choose. He wants to go home to Rosario. / "Did it hurt to die?" I finally ask. "Well," he says, "it hurt before I died." "Were you afraid?" "Of course. I listened for you, but you never came." My stomach tightens. "I wanted to be there. I couldn't get to you. Don't you think it hurt me to let you die?" He smiles. "I know," he says. We pass the ruins of a railyard. "Your grandfather is proud of you," he says. I look at him. The tears come. I try to stop them, but they force their way out anyway. "I don't want to be without you," I blurt. He looks at me for a long while, then taps me on the knee. "You've got to stop crying. You sound like a little girl." Then: "You aren't without me. Remember that." His eyes are clear. "Where are your glasses?" I ask. "Back on the side of the road," he says. "But that's all right. I won't be needing them now." "Were you cognizant at the hospital?" I ask. "Yes," he says with disgust. "I was trapped inside that damned dead body. I hated that." "I'm sorry, Papá," I tell him. He looks at me. "Don't be sorry. You waste so much time that you need for yourself." I nod. "I closed the coffin," I say. "Thank you. I didn't want to be on display." I touch his arm. "Papá, did you…did you see God?" He smiles at me and turns on the radio. / When I was fourteen, my father and I spent hours laughing in the night about nothing, nothing at all. / The car is red. The driver's seat is torn. A beehive swells inside it. Bees fly where his eyes used to be. They fly through the air that used to touch his lips. They walk on the bent wheel that cracked his ribs. They sit where he used to sit. A slow, warm cascade of honey spreads over the traces of demolition. It is gold. It catches the sunlight and reflects the clouds that move in its depths, minute and sparkling white. Droplets reflect the blue of the sky. They hint at the smile in my father's eyes.

Rosario, my earth

little town in which I learned to love

I dream of you, I miss you

thinking someday I'll return

Life took me from you,

but I never, never forgot you

my grandest illusion now

is to return to you once more

in the years of my nightfall

—Alberto Urrea
June 2, 1915 – January 10, 1977

BID FAREWELL TO
HER MANY HORSES

THE INDIANS WEREN'T TALKING to me. At Gabe's food store, they looked away from me when I bought a soda. There were three of them in there, plus Gabe's wife. Just to tweak them, I popped the lid right there and chugged it. Obviously, word had gotten around the res. They knew why I'd come, but they didn't know what to think of it. I felt bad enough. Their anger only made it worse.

Out in the light, I felt eyes watching me. The perfect smell of South Dakota was all over the street— I could fly in that air, fat with miles of prairie and storm clouds rushing from Nebraska to Iowa. I hunched up my shoulders. White boys visiting Pine Ridge can't help but remember all those cowboy movies. You listen for a whistling arrow, prepare for the mortal *thwack* when the shaft nails you between the shoulder-blades. Well, at least this white boy does. I probably had it coming.

I'd married one of the local girls. Her family didn't want her to marry me. They didn't want her to marry any white man. But we were wild for each other. We ran off to Deadwood, to a small chapel near the casinos. The minister was a Brule Sioux. She was Oglala. We took our honeymoon in the Black Hills—*Paha Sapa,* she told me, the center of the world. We stayed in a small motel below Mt. Rushmore. We bought those t-shirts that show four huge bare asses and say: "Rear View Mt. Rushmore." We laughed. Everything was funny.

Then the usual tough years. We went to California, both of us trying college. She tried writing to her family, but they were fighting mad. Our few visits back to the reservation were grim. I thought I was lonesome, but what happened to her heart out in California was a terror to see. I'd catch her looking up at the rattling palm trees sometimes, this look of sorrow on her face that almost looked like rapture.

And she couldn't get out of the bottle. They blamed me. I started to believe it, too. I'd fooled her away from her people, her world. Empty bottles, hidden at first beneath the sink, behind the apartment, clanked in the trash basket. She was quiet, as old-time Indian women are, and she wore a long braid in the old way. When she crashed the car, they say the braid was caught in the glass of the window. I don't know—I couldn't bear to look at the body. I sent her home on a train. It took me two days to drive out after her, and now I was burying my wife in the little graveyard near Our Lady of the Sioux. The headstone was already made. It said: "Joni Her Many Horses. Daughter, Sister. We Will Miss You. 1960-1990." They left my name off entirely.

DON HER MANY HORSES was Joni's oldest brother. Back in high school, when our teams played the Indians from Red Cloud, Don was a monster on the basketball courts. The way things were in those days, though, Indian boys didn't get too many victories. Even when they won. It was easy—the refs called them foul, or ejected them from the games for the least infraction. If they did win, they'd get their asses kicked after the game if we could find them...if there were more of us than them.

I made the mistake once of cracking wise to Don on the court. After one spectacular drive to the basket—when Don seemed to be floating over our heads for an impossible distance, then drove the ball down through the hoop so it caught no net, just streaked and hit the floor like a rock—I sidled up to him. I did what all us whites did in those days, dreaming of ourselves in Technicolor cowboy hats, our ideas as fixed as Mt. Rushmore, made sick in our hearts whenever we saw an Indian smile, certain somehow his smile took something away from our own souls.

"Hey, Chief," I said. "You got-um heap good medicine, huh? Y—"

Bang.

I was gone from the world.

When I came to in the shower room, it was like drifting out of deep purple water flecked with chips of fire. They brushed my skin as I surfaced. A million sweaty and hysterical dudes were glaring down at me. "Bobby!" they were shouting. "Bobby!" Don Her Many Horses was in jail, charged with aggravated assault. There had been trouble with the Indian kids, both teams slugging it out on the court. Cops had come in, sticks swinging. I listened to them babbling all about it as I stood in the shower, letting the water claw into my back and scalp. My left eye was tender as cube steak, and I could tell it was turning black.

"Shit," I said to no one in particular, "that brave sure can pack a punch!"

We all laughed and said the standard anti-Indian things you say. But I knew I was wrong. Here Don had made a spectacular play and I'd gone and opened my big ignorant mouth. I don't know that it changed my life. Maybe a little bit. I didn't turn all religious or anything over it.

DON HER MANY HORSES wasn't much interested in me at that point. He was slumped on the cot in his cell, nursing a collection of welts and eggs coming up all over his forehead. He had a rusty-bloody old rag soaked from the tin sink and held over one eye. I watched the water drops fall and hit the knee of his jeans. They shone bright for a second then sank in, spreading a color like grape juice as the denim darkened.

"Hi," I said.

"Fuck you, Bobby."

I ducked my head.

"Listen," I said. "I want to apologize for what happened."

He looked up at me. That eye was about swollen shut.

"Apologize, huh?" he said. He smiled a little. "All right. Go ahead."

"Sorry."

He stared at me with his one black eye. He didn't talk. That's one thing that drives you crazy with the Indians. Sometimes they just don't say anything. You don't know if they're thinking or laughing at you or what.

"I'm…," I said, "sorry. You know. About that wisecrack. And now you're in jail."

"Yeah, I can see that," he said.

Another pause.

"You got any chew?" he said.

I dug my tin of Copenhagen out of my back pocket and tossed it to him. Those boys, when they're not smoking, they're chewing. The women, too. Joni always had a little plug of peppermint tobacco pinched into her lip. I gave it up after high school. Don does it to this day.

I was thinking about leaving when he spoke: "You know what?" he said. "Next time I see you, I might have to take me a scalp. I might skin you, too. Brain-tan your hide and have me a new pelt to paint my winter count on. Hang your balls from my war lance. 'Course, everybody'd have to get up *real close* to see 'em."

There was nothing to say to that, so I left. I could hear his back-of-the-throat little laugh skittering around behind me as I walked down the hall. Damned Indians.

THE RESERVATION MEDICAL EXAMINER was taking care of Joni. I couldn't even look at the building as I drove by. I hooked south, out of Pine Ridge Village, heading toward White Clay, Nebraska. A couple of the guys driving around recognized me. Yellowhorse waved, one of the Red Clouds nodded imperiously at me, raising one hand as he coasted by in his old Ford pickup. They were burning a small pile of tires outside of town; the smoke rose like a mourning veil torn by wind. It angled away, fading to a haze that reached all the way out to the edge of the Badlands. The grass looked like Marilyn Monroe's hair. Horses swept through it like combs.

I was listening to KILI, "The Voice of the Lakota Nation." They were playing a twenty-megaton dirge by Metallica. It was followed by some Sioux music—the Porcupine Singers. If I listened long enough, they'd probably toss in some jazz and three Johnny Cash songs. There were supposed to be announcements of Joni's burial on there, but I never did hear any. I pulled up at the gate of the Her Many Horses spread. Don was walking a mottled gray horse in slow circles in front of their house. He ran his hand along the horse's flank; its skin jumped at his touch. It was limping. He glanced up at me and turned back to the horse.

I dropped the section of barbed wire fence that served as a gate and drove through.

"Close the gate!" Don hollered.

"I know, I know," I muttered to myself. Six dogs and four young horses headed for the opening, but I beat them to it. The horses veered away, suddenly innocent and fascinated by the sage plants beside the drive. The dogs charged me, then collapsed in the dirt, wagging their tails.

I drove up to Don, shut off the engine, and got out.

"She's sick," he said.

The old horse looked like rain clouds. I recognized her. They called her Stormy.

"That's Joni's old horse," I said.

Stormy put her giant old face next to Don's. He rubbed her long white upper lip. "That's okay," he murmured. "That's okay now."

"I'm sorry, Don," I said. "I did my best."

"Stormy's dyin'," he said. He had this disconcerting way of ignoring what I said. "I've been feeding her this medicine they give me down in Rapid. But them vets don't know shit about horses. You know it? She's got these tumors." He stroked Stormy's side. I saw that she was bloated, her abdomen distended like a barrel behind her ribs. "Now we got to kill her."

Stormy snorted.

"Go on now," he said to her. "Go ahead." She limped away.

"Them mother-effers."

"Don?" I said. "I'm sorry. About Joni. I mean, I'm sorry about Stormy too. But, what I mean. . . ."

One of the dogs nosed my crotch.

"Stop it," said Don. "I got a trailer pulled around back. You sleep there. Got food if you're hungry."

He lit a cigarette and walked away.

NIGHT ON THE RESERVATION is like night nowhere else. They say flying saucers visit the Sioux lands. Flying saucers and ghosts. When you're out there, there's a blackness that's deeper than black. The stars look like spilled sugar. You can hear the grass sometimes like water. Like somebody whispering. And the weird sounds of the night animals. Anything could happen. You get scared, and it's for a reason that hides behind the other reasons-behind the silence, and the coyotes, and the dogs barking, and the eerie voice of the owl. It's that *this is not your land. This is their land. And you don't belong.* A thousand slaughtered warriors ride around your camp, and you think it's the breeze. And they wonder why you're there.

I had the sleeping bag pulled over my head. It smelled like dust. My wife was lying five miles away, her breasts already dense as leather in death, her eyelashes intertwined, the perfect brown tunnels of her eyes sealed, the path within already forgotten. "Joni," I said. "Joni. Joni."

I MET HER AT NIGHT. Off the reservation, there are small joints scattered all along the roads. You can go in there for ice cream or burgers or beer. Lots of them sell Indian art and beads to the tourists, and a bunch of them still won't let an Indian in the door. The reservation folks knew which stores wanted them and which didn't.

We were in one that didn't. Six of the footballers from our school were in there with me. It was one of those dull nights. Red Cloud School had won the football game. They'd all been going down to see that *Little Big Man* movie, and they were all turned on. They were crazy-wild. Nobody could catch them.

Franklin Standing Bear's car broke down. He came walking up to the place from the road to Hot Springs. I watched him through the window, materializing out of the blackness. He paused in the parking lot, looking at us. His glasses glittered in the lights. I nudged one of the boys and pointed with my chin.

"Gaw-damn," he said.

We left our spoons sinking into our sundaes and gawked.

Franklin came in the door and dodged his head.

"More balls 'n brains," one of the football boys said.

Franklin went to the register and asked to use the phone. Sonny, the owner, had served in Korea with Franklin's dad, so he let him use the phone. But he told him he'd best get moving as soon as he was through.

We hustled out to the lot and waited for him, all jittery with crazy heat.

Franklin came out and our quarterback called, "Hey, boy!"

He put his hands up in front of him and said, "Not looking for trouble."

"You calling me a troublemaker?" the footballer asked.

"Look," Franklin said, "my car's busted down. That's all."

"You Indian boys did pretty good tonight," said the tight end. He looked like a chimp in the half light. All beady glittery eyes, stupid with lust. Jeez, this is how it begins, I thought.

"I don't know nothing about it," said Franklin. "I was over to Rosebud." He was drifting away.

"Rosebud," the first footballer said. "What kind of a faggot name is that, Standing Bear? You Indians all faggots or what? That why you got them ponytails?"

Franklin had a frozen smile on his face. He could see a freight train coming and he couldn't get out of its way.

"Let's go inside," I said. I tugged on the tight end's sleeve. "C'mon," I said.

Franklin Standing Bear spit on the ground.

"You know what?" he said. "You're just a bunch of low-life shit-lipped pud-pulling cow fuckers. I'm about fed up with your bullshit, so come on cowboys! Fuck it! *Hoka hey!*"

Oh man, I thought, he's doing his war cry. It was a good day to die. Franklin was in full-on warrior mode now.

The footballer grunted and charged at him. Franklin leaped about three feet high and kicked him precisely in the mouth. Franklin's glasses flew one way; blood and teeth flew the other. The footballer fell back, squealing, rolling on the blacktop with his fingers in his mouth. They closed in on Franklin, but he broke for the road. All our bootheels sounded like three horses crossing a highway. I didn't know what the hell I was doing. I was just running.

Two sets of headlights rounded the curve, and Franklin dodged between them. Indians poured out at us, like they were flying out of the light. One of them was Joni. She cornered me, waving a tire iron in my face. God, she was beautiful. She looked like a wolf; her small perfect teeth were bared, the muscles in her arms tight with rage. She was wearing a small choker. The cold had made her nipples stand up. She hissed and cussed at me. In her cowboy boots, she was taller than I was. I was sure she was going to knock my head loose. The sound of massacre was all around us. Don appeared beside Joni, grinning.

He was panting from the fighting, flushed and sweaty.

"Well, well," he said. "It's the Indian lover." He turned to Joni. "This here is a big Indian lover. Isn't that right, Bobby?"

Joni stopped waving the iron at me.

"Hey," said Don. "You come out here to *apologize?*"

There was a scattered rubble of white boys all over the road.

"I don't know," I said.

"You don't know," Joni taunted.

"I don't know." I was looking around.

"Looks like you picked the wrong place to be," she said. "That's for damn sure."

But they didn't do anything about it. We walked over to Don's car—a ferocious orange Chevy Impala—and Don drove us back to the edge of the lot and put me out. "Forgive us," he said in the phoniest arch-sounding accent, "if we shan't stop in for tea." They burned rubber. They were doing those manic *yip-yip* war cries as they sped away. I thought Joni waved good-bye, but I couldn't be sure.

We met again at a movie theater, by accident. I finally got down to see *Little Big Man,* and damned if I didn't wish I was a Sioux warrior. Somebody in the balcony kept pelting me with popcorn, though, but every time I turned around, there was nobody there. I finally jumped out of my seat and glared up there. Joni was laughing down at me. I blushed. After that, I kept thinking of the massacre at the Indian village —I kept thinking of a soldier shooting Joni in the back as she ran. It made me sick inside. I couldn't get the picture out of my mind. I was Dustin Hoffman, and I watched Joni run and die, run and die, in slow motion, extreme close up. The next time we saw each other, we were on.

MORNING. HORSES. They walked in patient circles around the trailer, snorting as they went past the screened window, trying to get a whiff of me without letting me know they were inspecting. Today was the burial. I got up, dragged on my jeans and a t-shirt, and stepped out. They trotted away with their ears bent back and their tails lifted. I went in the house quietly, but Don was already up, sitting at the table drinking coffee. He gestured to a skillet with three eggs and some bacon fried up. "Toast," he said, nodding to a stack of bread slices on a saucer before him. Silent, I got my breakfast and sat across from him. We stared at each other as I ate. Don's boy, Snake, was asleep on the couch, face down. Elinore Her Many Horses could be heard taking a shower. I was through eating. "Thanks," I said. "Put them dishes in the sink, hey?" he said. I did it. Then I waited my turn for the shower. Then it was time to go. I drove in my truck alone.

BETWEEN BREAKFAST and packing to leave, I can't remember the day. As soon as I saw the coffin, I was hit in the ribs, like a shovel swung by a batter. I kept focusing on breathing, dragging in air and letting it out slowly. My memory of everything else is a vague gray hum. I know that one of the Catholic Brothers from Red Cloud School led the service, and somebody played piano. I can't remember anybody's face, just the thought: breathe-breathe-breathe. Then we were standing on the steps of the church like a real family, and I shook hands with a faceless crowd. I didn't cry.

At the graveyard, I stood behind Don, about three paces, and watched the grass waver in the breeze. And afterward, I stopped at Red Cloud's grave to pay my respects to the old chief. Some Oglalas had left him tobacco ties, little sacred bundles in all the colors of the four directions. I asked him to take care of my woman out there, where she was new and maybe lost. I asked him to take her into his lodge and protect her until I could come for her. That's all I remember.

I ROLLED DON'S SLEEPING BAG carefully, taking pains to leave the little trailer neat. It was already late afternoon. We'd sat around inside, sipping coffee, murmuring. The television was on, turned down low. Snake stared at MTV, never looking up. Elinore sat beside me on the couch, and she periodically got up and fetched me cookies or more coffee, though I didn't ask for any. After tending to the sleeping bag, I stuffed my jeans into a small bag, and stepped outside and headed across Don's pasture, away from the trailers to the dark hump of the sweat lodge he'd built near a small stand of cottonwoods. I walked down to the stream that cuts through Don's eighty acres. There was one spot, one small, white-gravel pool where Joni and I made love.

It was perfectly matched to my memory, like a photo pinned inside my skull. I remembered every detail, even the giggling terror that Don, or their old man, Wilmer, would catch us at it. I stood there watching the wasps sip water at the edge of the pool, where the gravel gave way to mud. I half expected to see the double-seashell imprint of her bottom on the shore. Dragonflies tapped the water. I'd moved in her, minnows between our legs, tickling us. Bubbles came out of her body and ran over my sides.

There were tiny smears of black hair in her armpits. Her nipples were small and dark as nuts. She hardly had any hair on her body. Afterwards, as we lounged in the water, chewing leaves of spearmint that grew on the banks, she played with the hair on my chest. She scratched it: I could hear her nails scraping. I leaned up on one elbow, watching my seed rise from her and drift. It looked like a pearl column of smoke.

"Bobby."

I jumped. I looked around, feeling caught.

It was Don. He had a rifle on one shoulder. He was leading Stormy. They were dark against the sky. Huge.

"I...," I said. "I guess I saw a ghost."

Don nodded.

Stormy brushed flies away from her sides with lazy smacks of her tail.

"Wanna come?" he said, gesturing at the horse with his head.

I clambered up the bank and followed him. You could hear bees working the alfalfa and the sweetgrass. Stormy's limping gait played on the ground like a drumbeat. Don stared at the ground as we walked. She wheezed, the sound pitifully hollow and weak.

"Stormy thinks we're having fun," he said.

Her ears still turned to each sound. She watched a dove burst out of a small bush and fly away. She dipped her head at tall grasses, though she couldn't eat anymore. I noticed her legs trembling.

We took her over a small hillock, out of sight of the house and the other horses. "All right now," Don murmured. He worked the bit out of her mouth and pulled off the bridle. She worked her long yellow-brown teeth. She stared off.

Don cranked a round into the chamber. The lever sounded cool and final as it slid home.

"I tried," I said. He didn't look at me. "Whatever I did wrong, I loved your sister."

Don petted Stormy.

"I know it," he said. "Shit. I guess we all know it."

He raised the gun and fired into her head, behind her left ear. It was a sharp little *crack*, like a dry branch snapping. I jumped. She jerked her head straight up and fell. Her legs just vanished. Don had to dance out of her way when she dropped. The whole thing was unbelievable, some kind of trick. One of her hooves twitched; she groaned; then it was done. The silence was like a curtain in a play. You couldn't even see any blood. Don was standing there, the smoking rifle loose in his grip. I looked up at him—his eyes were closed, his head went back, and he began to sing.

He began to sing, quietly at first, but it grew louder as he went. Long mysterious Sioux sounds, Indian words that could have been going out to God, or to Stormy, or to Joni, there was no way of knowing. But his voice rose, became a haunted sound, a cry from some place else. I wanted to join him. I wanted to sing, to cry my pain and loss to Him—to the Grandfather, to the one she'd called *Wakan Tanka*. But I had no song, I had no prayer. I felt so small beside the voice of Don Her Many Horses.

I closed my eyes and stood with him. The good horse-smell still rose from Stormy. And he sang. I started to sob, it just tore out of me.

I thought I might fall down, but his hand gripped my upper arm to steady me. The wind sighed around us, and there were crows. Don kept singing, but he had slowed, enunciating carefully, and I realized he wanted me to follow. My voice was weak, at first, tentative, but I repeated the sounds. He waited until I grew strong in my song.

We sang for a long time, together. We sang until dark. We sang until I thought we would never find our way home.

AMAZING GRACE: STORY AND WRITER

AN AFTERWORD

Amazing Grace, how sweet the sound
That saved a wretch like me...

1.

STORIES, LIKE HUMAN BEINGS, gestate. Let me offer you an example: the place where the spark of my daughter's life was struck was a seven-walled third-floor room in the Auberge des Seguins in Provence. I was already past the threshold of forty and sure I would never father a child. But the writers in the workshop I was teaching had gone out for morning yoga and a hike to some Roman ruins. My wife Cinderella and I slept in.

The room was white, with thick medieval walls, its narrow windows covered with wooden shutters that could be flung open to the golden Mediterranean light. Dark old beams, one of them apparently charred by fire, crossed the ceiling. The one that angled over our bed was low enough that I repeatedly struck my head on it when I got up. We often joked that we should swing from it like naked monkeys.

On that sacred day, neither of us climbed onto the beam. The windows were open, and the mistral winds fluttered in from the hills. Birds called out in French. Bees bumbled into our room and wandered back out. Vine roses climbing the outer walls had blossoms as big as cabbages, and they cast up a reflected light of pink and orange as if a small flame had been ignited. And a fire did burn: the whole world was aflame. Everyone, on their first visit to France, must be as giddy as we were with its mystical heat.

Beyond our wooden windowframes and the roses, the walls were whitewashed, with broken sections revealing tawny stones piled like a million loaves of bread. The roofs were red tile. Beyond the buildings, the wildflowers on the hills were bright yellow, the trees were neon green, and the cliffs behind them were pastels and colored chalks. Roman stone bridges appeared between the fruit trees, so old that bushes and flowers grew from their roadways. The Auberge swimming pool was fed by an artesian well, and an adjacent pool held the trout the chefs fished out for supper every night. Nude Germans paraded around the emerald pool with their dogs.

One day, it rained in full sunshine. I remember it as being the day our child was conceived (as though she were an idea, a concept…a story) though I know it was not. It should have been, and my writer's mind insists that it was. Be that as it may, the cliffs beyond the Auberge were obscured by furling curtains of bright copper rain, dropping through the morning sun like beads. Blue sky, rosy cliffs, copper rain.

After a month in Provence, we took the bullet train to Paris. Cinderella was already feeling the effects of our little astral visitor. We lit candles in Notre Dame, and we rode carousels and ate chocolate croissants. We walked down the nocturnal Left Bank of the Seine and watched as the Tango Club danced by the water to scratchy Carlos Gardel records.

But mostly we slept.

WE HAVE ALL HEARD male writers claim that making a story or book or poem (or heavy metal song) is like a woman being pregnant and giving birth. Men are always busy appropriating details from women, as if we are too dense to come up with our own symbols and metaphors and meanings. I find the pregnancy allusion to be facile boy-talk. It's not quite as appalling as some lunk-head claiming he was "raped" in a bad business deal or a romantic dispute, but it chafes. After watching Cinderella be sick every morning, grow gravid with the weight of new life, then pay the physical and emotional toll of birth — after holding the gleaming child freshly risen from the womb and looking into her ancient eyes, seeing a frightening recognition in them, and a tightly-held secret — I will never again liken it to *typing*.

Rosario Teresa, aka "Chayo," is no novel.

Still, the Great Events of story and baby have something in common. The story, like Chayo, seems to have come into the dark of the compact interior universe. It sparked, then throbbed, then subdivided in my head. Something came from (almost) nothing. Loaves and fishes. Water into wine.

If you look at miracles, they always accelerate Nature. Loaves did not come from stone or thin air—they came, like they would in the field, from other loaves. Wheat makes more wheat. Wine didn't come from dust—wine came from water, which is where wine comes from. Rain passes through the fabulous machinery of vines and twigs and grapes to make itself into wine. Every glass of Welch's grape juice or room temperature Merlot is a little Biblical miracle in a glass.

At the same time that we were exploring Provence—the woods of the Luberon, the Saturday market in Apt, the quays of Marseille with their sly octopi reaching out through the slats of the fishermen's crates, the ice cream stands of Avignon—a story was pulsing in my head. It had nothing at all to do with France. It was a vision of pre-revolutionary Mexico, of the Sonoran desert and Yaqui wars and an ancestor of mine they'd called a saint.

I'd been working on this story for many years. Over a decade. Most of the writing of it was not writing at all: it was research, investigation, dream-time, travel. Much of it was spent sweating in the driver's seat on haunted Southwestern highways. Crouching over old files in archives. Sitting in deserts or sweat-lodges or little Mexican houses with women and men of power, being shown things I was not later allowed to tell. But, you see, it was all writing, though nothing composed hit paper.

Even if, at the moment, you can't sit down and do the gruntwork of stringing verbs and nouns together, you are writing. It is a way of seeing, a way of being. The world is not only the world, but your personal filing cabinet. You lodge details of the world in your sparkling nerve-library that spirals through your brain and coils down your arms and legs, collects in your belly and your sex. You write, even if you can't always "write."

However, writers write. Active, not passive.

I HAD POKED AROUND at Harvard, in Tijuana, in Tucson, in Tubac. In El Paso and Juárez and Culiacán. In Mexico City and Cuernavaca and the reservation. And now I found myself in France.

I was stalled—perhaps not writer's block, but a near standstill. The story would not come. I knew the material, but I could not see it. In the Auberge, that morning, as Cinderella took a shower, I lay on my back and watched the light on the ceiling. Looked at the walls. Looked at the doors.

Looked.

Thick white walls, wobbly and off-plumb, showing trowel-marks and streaks. It looked like adobe. The roof beams looked like vigas. Wooden shutters, blue wooden chairs, crooked wooden doors. Even the fabulous roses. It looked so...Mexican.

I suddenly saw the saint's bedroom in my mind. Chayo sparkled inside Cinderella's belly, and the lost white bedroom of my ancestor sparkled in my skull. The tales had begun.

As I write this, Chayo constantly interrupts me, waving books over her head and shouting, "TORY! TORY!" We have already read *Dirt Is Delightful* and *One Bear Two Bears* and *Green Eggs and Ham*. I keep trying to get back to work, but she insists. I mutter, "Damn it, Chayo." And she yells: "Dammet! TORY!"

Story will not be denied.

2.

WE WERE THE ONLY family in our particular corner of the 'hood with a library. We were certainly the only apartment in the housing project with Dickens and Steinbeck on a book shelf. I was not only invited to read: I was *expected* to read. Reading was my responsibility, in English and Spanish. Like many poor kids before me, I was given the best gift anyone could hope for—a library card.

On Saturdays, my mother and I would take the #11 bus downtown. I'd haul my stack of the week's books inside and come back out with a new armload. I was a millionaire. The only thing that matched the hush of the library was the mysterious quiet of the church, where I got dizzy on incense and the Latin of the Old Mass. In the library, I might have been rich, but in church I wanted to be a saint. I yearned to see God, and I looked for Him everywhere. I'm still doing it.

From the library, we'd walk over to Woolworth's, where I'd get a hot dog and some orange soda, then we'd look at the parakeets and goldfish. A free zoo. Then we'd catch the bus and I'd be home in time for Moona Lisa's monster show on Channel 10.

Monsters were as important to my writing mind as the books. It took me a long time to understand this—the bus ride, the bums in the shadows on Broadway, the scary men's toilet in the basement of the library, the hushed stacks, the Woolworth's hot dog counter and the pet section, these were all things that pushed my eyes open a little more. I wanted to catch them and never let them go. This might be a definition of what writing is. It's like mounting butterflies. (Go, Nabokov!) Tom Sawyer and the Crab Monsters, Huck Finn and King Kong. Moona Lisa and my dad's Pedro Infante records. I had an undefined sense of myself as a historian. I was somehow responsible for the details. I think this is true of all the writers I know: writers attend, which is different from seeing. Pay attention! (In Spanish, that great contrary language, you *lend* attention, which is perhaps more accurate.)

I was in the world of Ali Baba and Theseus. In my mind, I rode

Pegasus out of the sky and swept Roxanne Bambino out of the playground while all my enemies gaped and sputtered. I was hooked. Even now, I feel like more of a fan than an author. I sit up way too late reading the latest James Lee Burke, as I once hid under the covers with a flashlight after bed time, reading the latest Andre Norton space adventure.

A parade of fictions and fictionists started, a long procession with much pulp and great fancy, hard-boiled prose and mystical claptrap, literary maneuvers and scary monsters. Even cowboys and metafiction. How could you ever read enough? They marched through, waving their banners, charting an unlikely pattern: E.E. Doc Smith, Kenneth Robeson, Ray Bradbury, Theodore Sturgeon. Then Wilbur Smith, Robert Ruark, Edgar Allen Poe, Ambrose Bierce, Kate Willhelm, H.P. Lovecraft. Leonard Cohen, Richard Brautigan, Robert F. Jones, Kurt Vonnegut, Ishmael Reed, Richard Fariña. Ursula Le Guin, Gabriel Garcia Márquez, Borges, Cortázar, Doris Lessing. The world accelerated. Coover, Barthelme, Stephen King. How could I list them all for you? In what mad order? Cervantes, Tolstoy, Rulfo. Steinbeck and Hemingway. Rudolfo Anaya. Tom McGuane, Ed Abbey, Jim Harrison (I found a pile of Harrison's books in that same downtown Woolworth's, years later, all of them going for $1.00 each). Kerouac. Flannery O'Connor, Eudora Welty, John Irving, Breece D'J Pancake, Raymond Carver. McMurtry and McCarthy. Linda Hogan, Leslie Silko, Louise Erdrich. Ernest Gaines.

I can't believe how many of my students don't read. They want to be writers, but they haven't read anything at all. They have looked at book covers, which usually allows them enough expertise to sneer, but they haven't read the books. How many young poets "don't like" poetry? How many fiction writers don't know Dennis LeHane from Nevada Barr?

Maybe the violence on the street made me read. It was certainly wiser to stay inside with Doc Savage than it was to brave the vatos and bloods outside. It became a habit, this world of writing and story. Later, of course, writing itself became a habit.

More, however, than the books and the monster movies and the rich details of barrio life and the exultations of education, another factor ignited writing in me.

It was the spoken word.

ALL MY WRITER FRIENDS are snoops.

One day, on the Red Line subway, going from Cambridge to Boston, a fellow leaped out of his seat near the Charles Street station and made an announcement. I was lucky enough to be there with my journal, and I jotted it down. This is what he said:

"I bribe indiscriminately! I'm famous for that. Listen to four hours of X, and you'll know what I am. I'm a communist, and I'm a fucking bore! You've got to change the metric system, Olga! At least you're honest. And they wanted to press charges against Elvis Presley at the Law School, Harvard University. *Exactly one million dollars!*"

Then the doors opened and he jumped off the train. It was June 1, 1984. I was happy all day — overjoyed by his madness and by my good fortune to capture his soliloquy.

Will it find its way into a story? You bet.

I WAS ALWAYS this way. As a child, I was used to listening to adults. My mother and father fought when they thought I was asleep. As the family historian, I had to listen. As the family saint, it was my duty to study each tempest and find ways to outmaneuver their ever-impending divorce. I didn't know what would happen to us when our family finally, irrevocably, ruptured. But I knew, because Sister Bernita had told me, that my parents would go to Hell if they separated. It was only my attention to their details that kept them from burning.

On the few occasions when my folks threw parties, I'd lie in bed and listen to the astounding hilarity of adults tipping back a few, firing up their Pall Malls, and being naughty as the Bert Kaempfert records played. "Red Roses for a Blue Lady" mixed with off-color jokes in Spanish and English. My father's favorite joke, abut a man with an elephant trunk for a penis, ended with him crying, "How do I like it? Every time I pass a peanut vendor, it grabs a peanut and shoves it up my ass!"

I know for a fact, though, that story and writing entered my life full-force with the tall tales about my father's hometown. It was a little town on a river. Rosario, Sinaloa.

3.

PEOPLE FROM ROSARIO are crazy about their town. There are Rosario clubs all over the place, where folks from Rosario sit around and congratulate each other for being from Rosario. Wherever two or more are gathered in Rosario's name, there will Rosario be also. They are so crazy about their little town that they can convince you it's more special, strange, sexy, and beautiful than any other town. People from Rosario will claim that my daughter, Rosario, is named after their town. She isn't—she's named after my godmother—but you'll never convince them of it.

My cousin Fausto, for example, would come visit us in San Diego and, though he was a polyester-wearing hick from a dinky Mexican villa, he was able to spin tales of lizards, breasts, tequila, whores, bras, fights, ghosts, bulls, nipples, dances, cleavage and...did I mention breasts? Rosario, in Fausto's mind, was the center of the universe. Jimi Hendrix had nothing on the guitar player who strummed in the local whorehouse, "El Club Verde Para Hombres." Carlos Santana? "Nothing special," Fausto would sniff. "I've heard better in Rosario." And everybody in Rosario was having wild sex, Fausto most of all. He wore hand-cut huaraches made by a guy who kept pots of fermenting human dung with which to tan the leather.

Everything was bigger, better, tastier, awfuller in Rosario. We'd get in the car, parked in California's July sun, and the heat blast would wilt us all. Fausto would say, "You feel this heat? It's hotter than this in Rosario!"

MY FATHER AIDED AND ABETTED these tales with tales of his own. Pedro Infante, after all, came from Rosario. Gilbert Roland fished for shrimp an hour from town. The Grand Lola Beltran came from Rosario. Names of obscure Rosarenses (as folks from Rosario are called) assumed legendary status in our home: Carlos R. Hubbard; El Guero Astengo; Pedro Borrego y la Banda Orquesta Borrego; Crispin Ugalde; Ernesto James, our neighbor in Tijuana who'd get drunk and shoot his pistol at the moon, sending us all scattering till he calmed down. The guy with the coolest nickname on earth came from Rosario: El Quemapueblos—The Man Who Burns Down Villages.

Rosario became, I suppose, my own Macondo. It was a place that existed more in stories and fantasies than in the real world. I lived among other people's memories. Far from being a hot and occasionally stinky subtropical town of 10,000 souls, it became a font of myth and lies and outrageous tales and pride and romance. And when I finally visited Rosario, on several extended stays over the years, it was still a fiction. I saw everything there as if it were narrated by someone else, for it had been. There was no Rosario; there were only Rosario stories. Every small street, every cobble, was written or whispered, and all I had to do was walk around and say, "Yes, I remember."

MY FIRST VISIT was in 1970. My father and I took a bus. The stewardess, Berta, had a wine stain birthmark on her cheek. Her hair was carefully arranged over that cheek, giving her an air of mystery that kept me awake at night. She brushed me with her hip every time she went past. I had never had a woman brush me with her hip.

We were accosted one night by bandidos in a pickup, firing guns in the air. During the day, a big blowsy Texan woman sat beside the bus driver (who later died, I heard, in a big wreck) and insulted Mexico. "Look at those cows," she said. "They're starving!" He said, "What cows, lady? Those are Mexican rabbits!" And my father had given me a copy of *The Godfather*, which was about the most insane thing I had ever read. How could story not find me? The bus trip alone was a Malcolm Lowry novel.

I chased the housegirls in my uncle's home, climbing over tables as they laughed and screamed, hoping for just one kiss. I slept naked in the heat. One morning, the house girl, Carmelita, came in my room. I pulled up my sheet to cover my top half, and the bottom of the sheet uncovered my bottom half. She said, "Is that the way you say 'good morning' in California?"

There was a cross-dresser who lived near a statue in a traffic roundabout, and they called him "The Flower of the Monument" (La flor del monumento). I loved him, and he loved me, or at least he batted his eyes at me. And the other famous gay man in town sold women's shoes out of his bedroom. They were both tolerated, though the he-men of the town told me hideous stories of manly retribution against gays: they claimed to cut the tails off pigs and dry them, staked out straight on boards, in the tropical sun. Then, when the tails were stiff, they'd hold down the men and shove the tails in their behinds—the worst part being that the bristles pointed backwards, so that when they pulled the tails back out, the hairs would open up and tear the men apart.

Because I was a blonde boy, one of these manly men, Chuy El Gordo, decided he had to rape me. A Chinese-Mexican karate fighter named El Chino Cochino beat him up. We drank rum and hugged each other and pledged eternal brotherhood. I never saw him again. His pal, a guy called Fu Manchu, taught me to smoke, which was appropriate, because his nickname had a nickname, "El Fuma," which basically meant "the smoker." He hated my Spanish. "You talk like a girl," he said. He also said I smoked like a girl. He taught me to suck it down and let it out through my nose. I left smoking in Sinaloa and never touched a cigarette after that.

Other nicknames in the crowd were Taras Bulba, Dracula, Frankenstein, El Piochas, El Tuerto, and several Gordos.

THE MOST LOVELY GIRL I ever saw was deaf, and I was smitten with her when she'd come in my uncle's stationery store to buy paper or pencils, and we invented an impromptu sign language to communicate. Tachito, the village maniac, rode a red and rattling bike all over town, blowing one of those "a-oo-gah!" horns at everybody. He wore rags tied around his head, and he carried spoiled vegetables in the basket on the front of his bike, hoping to sell them to somebody, anybody. Tachito, like La Flor, seemed to love me too, and he pursued me on his bike, going "A-oo-gah! A-oo-gah!" right behind me and giggling. He gave me an eggplant. Then, one day, he gave me a baby snapping turtle. It immediately attached itself to my thumb. We put it in a tub of water, where it sank to the bottom and lurked like a dropped coin, waiting for more fingers to bite.

ONE DAY, I SAT in my uncle's store talking to my friend Maria de los Angeles. We had both seen the dementedly violent surrealist film "El Topo," and we were debating its merits and failings. I looked up and realized we were suddenly in the middle of a crowd of young women. I said, "What's going on?" Maria said, "No boy has ever asked us our opinion about a movie."

I got drunk for the first time there.

I also caught paratyphoid and nearly died. I sank into a world of visions and hallucinations. By the time I was ready to write about Rosario, I didn't know if my cousin Irma had ever walked across the sky, or if I had merely seen it in a fever.

4.

ONE OF THE GREATEST CHARACTERS in Rosario's history was Pancho Mena. Pancho Mena had declared himself the practical joke king of all Mexico. And the people didn't want a practical joke king. I've written about him elsewhere, and I'll no doubt write more about him later. (His cruellest and greatest joke is recorded in *Nobody's Son.*) But the tales of Mena's depredations had me rolling on the ground as a kid. Mena tales were my favorite Rosario stories by far — even better than the endless stories of sexual conquest.

They combined, in my mind, with Steve Allen's book, *Is It Bigger Than A Breadbox?* and with the old "Blooper" LP's you could buy for a dollar at the drugstore. I was caught in a paroxysm of pranksterism, wacky exploits that kept me in stitches. Everything, for a while, was funny. I thought I was crazy. I insisted that I was crazy. Salvador Dali and Pancho Mena and Curly of the Three Stooges were my heroes!

Mena shaved his head, for example, and bought a bike, which he painted black. Then he coated his head with flour, dressed in black clothes, tied a sheet around his neck, and rode the bike downhill through the center of town, caterwauling and gibbering. He was, of course, enacting our favorite demon/ghost, La Llorona, and terrified Rosarenses hid under beds and clutched rosaries as he yowled by their doors.

Then there was the night he happened upon a wake and decided to steal the body and stand it up against a friend's door at midnight and knock until the door opened....

This sort of thing was a daily occurrence during the reign of King Mena. He courted disaster and nearly went to prison a few times. Once, he killed a woman by accident.

A friend of his had died, and the Mass was well-attended and heart-rending. Mena, since his head was already shaved, and since he had a bunch of flour left over from the Llorona Incident, decided it would be a good idea to hide behind the altar and pretend he was the ghost of the dead man. He picked his moment, too. In the middle of the service, as the women started wailing the dead man's name, Mena stood up and bellowed, "What do you want!" In the ensuing stampede, a woman died of a heart attack. Various tellers insist it was either the dead man's wife or his mistress.

Much of what happens in my story, "Mr. Mendoza's Paint-brush," is basically true. As is Mr. Mendoza himself. He's just a slightly transformed Pancho Mena. It's not too long a hop from practical joke king to graffiti king. The implied cultural criticism and anarchy are the same.

I guess I was thinking something like: what if Pancho Mena had been an Old Testament prophet?

AT HARVARD, WE USED to teach the "Indirect Means of Telling a Story," later reduced to the sound-bite dullness of "Imagery." One of my brilliant freshmen named it "The Understory." That's what I like, the dark stirrings in the basement of the story. No, not the basement, the boiler room. Not even the boiler room: the engine room. Down there, where it's cobwebby and dusty, oily and stinky, weird and a little frightening, that's where the jars with the meta-phors and similes and symbols and dreams are stored. Rosario, as you can see, was certainly imbued with understory.

We always make use of the iceberg illustration in writing work-shops. You know, one eighth of the iceberg is above water—much like a story—and seven eighths lurk under the surface, waiting to sink the Titanic. That seems altogether too passive to me, so I like to teach the snapping turtle example: we see a fragment of shell and part of his sneaky old head above the waves, but the big body and the powerful legs are dangling beneath, ready to drive that turtle at alarming speeds. Engine rooms and turtles. An atomic turtle provided by Tachito, the town lunatic.

5.

MY UNCLE CARLOS owned the radio station in Rosario and the movie house and the newspaper. He refused to play rock and roll records, so I had stacks of discarded radio station 45's in the house, and I spent hours in the deep heat rocking the geckoes off the walls. Led Zeppelin, the Byrds, Creedence, The Sons of Champlin. The family was aghast at "Born on the Bayou," Mexicans having never heard a man screaming like John Fogerty unless he was exhorting revolutionaries to burn down some building and kill all the land owners. They used to call him "El enojado"—The Mad Guy. In their opinion, "Sugar Sugar" by the Archies was the kind of "rocanrol" music kids should be listening to.

My cousin Jaime made cricket chirps with his mouth and kept me up all night singing "Bungalow Bill" and "Rocky Raccoon." The theater had bats in the rafters and showed a weirdly dubbed version of John Wayne's *The War Wagon*. Tia Cristina, the torta-lady who sold these evil chile sandwiches under the screen, for some reason christened me "Pig-Foot" (pata de cochi), which is a nickname I will gladly bear with pride. Nobody got pregnant; there were no fistfights; nobody left home forever, facing the dangerous road and the distant future. Except maybe me, alone and feverish in a big bus with a baby iguana in the luggage rack.

THE GOOD PEOPLE of Rosario are still infected with stories and jokes. You never know when a new astonishment or prank is coming. Awful things: a boy was run over by a gas truck, and, as my uncle reported in his paper, they had to pry the boy's flesh out of the treads of the tires with a knife. Eerie stuff: my friend Angel is a cop in town. The Rosario jail has no cells. A Federal Judicial cop showed up one night and told Angel he was transporting some bank robbery suspects in his car, but he was tired and had to sleep. He needed to leave them with Angel for the night. "We have no cell," Angel said. "That's all right," the cop replied. "I already shot them. Just stack the bodies in the corner."

Jokes: the Limon family has apparently gone quite mad. They have a picnic table in their back yard with an invisibly thin depression carved in the wood. They invite visitors to sit there without telling them the depression is full of water. Then they all laugh at the victims' wet butts. And they have a recliner chair with some kind of engine in it that makes the chair go off like the mechanical bull in a Texas bar. Woe to the poor soul who rests in this seat.

A shopkeeper in town pays a destitute old hag to live in his back storage room. When a new victim comes in the store, he tells the mark that the store is haunted and that he's afraid to go in the back. Then he asks the visiting "person of reason" to fetch a can for him. The old women jumps up and yells, "Boo!"

IT SEEMS TO ME that everywhere is Rosario. Or it should be. Not the real-world Rosario, which is, after all, a small place that won't play Bob Dylan records. But the inner, understory Rosario. Everywhere I go seems like a visit to Disneyland. Maybe it's because I never thought I'd go anywhere.

A SMALL ANECDOTE about "inspiration": although it deals with multiple levels of oppression, the story "First Light" was actually inspired, somehow, by a ridiculous scene that took place in Mazatlan. I took my uncle to the first Kentucky Fried Chicken restaurant in Sinaloa. It had just opened, and it was a media sensation. ("Kay-tooooooooooooooky Frize Sheeekuns!" the deejays shouted on the radio.) We went in and I ordered for the family, since they had never seen such food. When we sat down at the table to eat, I noticed my uncle piling cole slaw on the chicken. He'd pick up his drumstick, and the slaw would fall off. He'd sigh, put down the sheekun, and pile on the slaw again. And it would fall off. This W.C. Fields routine went on until he threw down his chicken and scattered the slaw with his plastic spoon and cried, "This is the worst damned salsa I've ever seen!"

6.

"FATHER RETURNS From the Mountain" is the only fiction in *Six Kinds of Sky* that is utterly true.

Aside from being the account of my father's awful death (a strictly "non-fiction," whatever that is, account can be found in *Across the Wire*), it is also my last gasp of fascination with metafiction. Anti-story was big business when I was in college, and I loved the stuff. When I grew up, I wanted to be Robert Coover or Donald Barthelme. I was writing all these intellect-addled stories about little people living inside concrete bricks in a garden while a genius college student types in the kitchen, and other people being dead but knowing it, and a poor man who breathes in a mote of dust that happens to be the spore of a parasitic humanoid that grows inside him and replaces him, and fellows living out all 100 alternate possibilities of any given moment at once, and stuff that was listed from A to Z. With little chunks of story attached to each letter. "D. A feather drops from the sky. Fallen from the wing of a hawk, it settles unseen behind the jade trees."

I was in a writing workshop taught by the inimitable Lowry Pei. Ursula K. LeGuin was on her way from Portland to take over the reins. Great hustling and maneuvering overtook the student body at UCSD, everyone trying to get in at once to be in the presence of the Great Woman. We had to audition, and to do so, we had to submit a piece of writing.

My dad had just been killed, driving home from—where else?—Rosario. I was trying to force my way through my senior year. I was studying writing and poetics with Dr. Donald Wesling. And the Good Doctor didn't like the stuff I was writing about my father. He called me into his office and said, "You are trying to hurt me with this writing. You are hysterical. If you want me to feel anything, you'll have to get control of yourself. Get control of your work. Tell it coldly. Let me feel it for myself."

I didn't like it at the time, but it was one of the best bits of advice I ever got.

I typed "Father Returns" on a mimeograph stencil and ran it off for Pei's class. Pei took the stencil and gave it to Le Guin. I got in. A couple of years later, Ursula published it in an anthology. It was my first sale.

It was a Pocket Books paperback called *Edges*, and my gang that hung out all night at Winchell's Donuts playing guitars and meeting donut-munching girls trooped down to the bookstore and stood before the shelf, gawking. It was the first time I had ever seen my work anywhere other than my kitchen table. One of the guys, a Mescalero Apache classical violinist who, on a bad acid trip, had been chased down the street by a giant Taco Bell taco, was the only man in the group noble enough to buy one. Note to readers: don't ask writers for free books—buy them. He asked me to sign one, and as I was signing some wise-ass thing like "Watch out for tacos!," a woman stopped me and actually asked, "Are you somebody?"

I was able to say, "Why, yes. I am somebody."

SOMETIMES THE DEAD speak to you. Maybe not you, but they speak to me. Though, if you're a writer, they're whispering. For comfort's sake, take what I'm saying figuratively.

After he died, my dad made a series of appearances. He appeared to all kinds of people, even people I would not have allowed him to visit if I'd been writing the script. I put those visits in the story. They took the form of strange dreams. I reported them as narrative fact.

In the last dream, my dad shook me awake. It was dawn. "Come with me," he said. I got up. He took my hand and pulled me through the wall. We flew to the corner of Clairemont and Dakota Drives. There, his dead friends from Rosario were waiting for me. Among them was the famous Pedro Borrego, from the Banda Orquesta Borrego. And by gum, there was Pancho Mena. Aside from being the practical joke king of Mexico, he was a wandering violinist who made money playing ballads and serenades. These jolly dead men stood around me and played ghastly 1940's Mexican rooty-tooty music as the sun rose and the cars faded like phantoms in the road.

It was a small blessing, a touch of grace in a dark hour.

THAT'S ABOUT IT. The book is some kind of downward spiral. It starts out all full of jokes and ends in fire and poverty and death. It reflects an early fascination with escape, then deals with returning, then staying put and dealing with it, whatever it is.

I always remember what Neal Cassady, Kerouac's old buddy once said: "Grace Beats Karma."

Yeah, man!

Grace beats Karma.

Grace beats fiction.

Grace beats death.

Grace beats memory.

Grace beats oppression.

Grace might even beat tenure!

It's so true. All these tales are really about grace. The story of writing is about Grace. Grace vs. Fate. God's hand reaching in and stirring the pot. Six kinds of sky: six kinds of life: six versions of God: six kinds of grace.

Without grace, I, for one, am nothing.

LUIS ALBERTO URREA was named by *Bloomsbury Review* as one of its "10 Young Writers to Watch." His book *Across the Wire*, which depicts life at the edges of the dumps in Tijuana, is in its 11th printing. After doing relief-work on the border for six years, Urrea taught Expository Writing at Harvard. His fiction, non-fiction, and poetry are widely anthologized, most recently in *The Late Great Mexican Border* and in *The Best American Poetry*. A novelist, essayist and poet, he has received the Christopher Award, the Colorado Center for the Book Award, the Western States Book Award for Poetry, and the American Book Award, among others. With his wife Cindy and his three children, he lives and teaches in Chicago.